M+O
4EVR

M + O
4EVR

Tonya Cherie Hegamin

Houghton Mifflin Company
Boston 2008

www.houghtonmifflinbooks.com

The text of this book is set in Palatino.

Library of Congress Cataloging-in-Publication Data
Hegamin, Tonya.
M+O4EVR / written by Tonya Hegamin.
p. cm.
Summary: In parallel stories, Hannah, a slave, finds love while flee-
ing a Maryland plantation in 1842, and in the present, Opal watches
her life-long best friend, Marianne, pull away and eventually lose her
life in the same Pennsylvania ravine where Hannah died.
ISBN-13: 978-0-618-49570-2
[1. Best friends—Fiction. 2. Friendship—Fiction. 3. Death—Fiction.
4. Family life—Pennsylvania—Fiction. 5. Lesbians—Fiction.
6. Slavery—Fiction. 7. Maryland—History—1775-1865—Fiction.
8. Pennsylvania—Fiction.] I. Title. II. Title: M plus O forever.
PZ7.H35885Maao 2008
[Fic]—dc22

Printed in the United States of America
MP 10 9 8 7 6 5 4 3 2 1

To whom do I owe the symbols
of my survival?
—Audre Lourde, *Zami: A New Spelling of My Name* (1983)

If it were possible,
I would gather the race in my arms
and fly away with them.
—Ida B. Wells, *Memphis Diary* (1887)

Just having thoughts of Marianne
quickest girl in the frying pan.
—Tori Amos, "Marianne" from *Boys for Pele* (1996)

REWARD

LAST SEEN THIS SEPTEMBER 14, in Goshen Township, Chester County. Answers to the name "HANNAH." Ran away from plantation of the Honorable Silas Forkswell, Dorchester County, Maryland. Described by her Master as a handsome dark-skinned wench of solid, full build, about 15–17 years of age, with a small mole on her right cheek. Seemingly docile, she has a crafty wit and a deceitful manner. Possibly lurking in the woods. May or may not be traveling alone. Anyone capturing and securing said wench or returning her to her Master shall receive a $30 reward, and $20 for the capture of any of her abettors.

ONE

"HEY, BABY. Got us some pretty little horsies to ride," Marianne said, sauntering up to me with her most wicked smile, like nothing had ever changed. I'd been folding Gran's underwear at the Drip 'n' Drop, floating on the flowery scent of warm dryer sheets. Marianne was wearing her homecoming crown, tilted to the side of her head—a drunken princess. Hair and makeup courtesy of the night before. At least she looked like she had on a different wife-beater and jeans than usual. Well, they didn't have any stains or graffiti on them, so they seemed different. Still, she was a shining star, the tiara on her head a twinkling remnant of the comet she'd just hijacked to get here. Her granddaddy's old hunting coat looked straight off the runway, instead of straight out the garage. I couldn't figure what made her trashy and brilliant at the same time. She wasn't even that pretty, but everybody knew she was hot.

I dropped the Hanes Her Way, put my brown hand in her yellow one, and away we go . . .

🌿 🌿 🌿

Flying out of town in her Mamm's rusty El Camino, blaring Sheila E. with the windows down. It was like thirty degrees with no sun in sight, but we never put the windows up. I played a little game—closed my eyes and tried to see all the houses and trailers and dead brown fields in my head; then I opened them again, to see if what was in my head was the same as outside. I almost knew this town by heart. Marianne was playing bongos on the steering wheel, screaming the words to "The Glamorous Life." At each turn we made, I envisioned us in a horrible collision, our mangled bodies all over the road and the mutant hybrid car/truck flipping dolphin-esque through the air. Another little game I liked to play: What would my last words be? More important, what would M's last words to me be? Would she finally tell me she loved me, or just say something they'd print on the first page of the yearbook? Besides her homecoming coup, there wouldn't be much to write about this year—we'd just lost the big game to the Stetson Stallions, 32 to 6. Go, rowdy Raccoons. Marianne looked over at me and flashed her pearly whites, her hair wildly whipping about her face like so many snakes. I told myself not to fall into the pit of her, but she reached over and squeezed my thigh, making me scream inside. I wanted to throw myself out the car. I wanted to throw myself into her. I bit my nails instead.

"She wants to lead the glamorous life . . . Without love . . ." she sang offkey. Marianne was like that, offkey to everybody but herself. She sang like it was the last song in the world.

We turned in to the gravel drive leading to what used to be the mill about five miles outside of town. I didn't know what we were doing here, but as usual, I was along for the ride. Pulling up to the back door, she honked the horn like a madwoman. She shut off the ignition but left the music on. M winked at me as she got out the car, still singing, rocking her head back and forth, jostling the sparkly tiara; somehow it stayed on. Then she went and stretched herself out on the hood of the car, like some glam-rock video skeeza. The steam from her hot breath hung around her head—her very own private fog machine.

The door to the old mill slid open and out came a dude I recognized as the quarterback from the Stallions. I wondered for only a half second where Marianne's boyfriend, Brock, was (I called him Block, as in Blockhead, but he thought it was because he's the center for the rabid Raccoons), when this guy jumped on M and shoved his tongue down her throat. Lucky me with the front-row seat. My disgust turned to pure revulsion as he opened his eyes and stared straight into my face while kissing and groping Marianne. I pulled my green baseball cap over my eyes and put my foot up on the windshield glass to cover his bloated, ugly face.

When they finally got off the car and I'd chewed most of what was left of my fingers, there was a nice size 9 shoe-print on the glass. Mr. Peek-a-Boo Quarterback went inside the mill, pointing his forefinger back at her like a gun, his thumb cocked. What a cowboy. M rolled off the hood and leaned into the open window on my side, touching my cheek with the nail of her red-polished but mostly chipped pinky finger. The pads of her fingers were puckered from the cold, and I could feel the uneven wrinkles; she wore only thin little black gloves with half the fingers cut off.

"Let's go, girl," she purred. "I promised you a ride."

She smelled like booze, smoke, and, well, funk. Once upon a time she had smelled of fresh earth and tasted like blackberries.

"What happened to the Block?" I asked, suddenly feeling like he was some sort of fallen comrade.

M shrugged and stood up, lip curled in boredom and disgust. I tried not to care that she hadn't brushed her teeth in a while. "I think he fell asleep in some field somewhere. He was pouting too much anyway. So I picked up these yahoos for my amusement." She opened the car door and held out her hand to me again. I just wanted to look at her forever, her hand out like that. M sniffed, wiping her nose with the back of her other hand.

"C'mon," she said with a hint of what I wanted to believe was pleading. "You gotta celebrate with me! I'm the first black Homecoming Queen in all a Kilmee County. It's a historic event. Who knows—maybe I'll even win Prom Queen. Then I'll be the Queen 'Coon!"

She laughed a little too hysterically at her own racist joke about herself. I thought to remind her she was only half black, but I didn't really want to quibble. She only remembered her dad was black when she felt like it, when it was convenient, like when she wanted to have a reason for feeling alienated, important, or "down." Otherwise she pretended to forget it and hoped everybody else did, too. She did that a lot, not just about her race. I sighed, stood up, and stretched. Would I ever get tired of these reindeer games?

She smiled, winked as I took her hand again.

❧ ❧ ❧

Inside the mill was a reenactment of several of my worst nightmares: a bunch of drunken white boys in football jerseys. Not that it was twelve in the afternoon or anything. Not that they were all in various states of prone or perpendicular consciousness. Not even that they were all still congratulating themselves for a stupid game that they won almost twenty-four hours ago by slapping, punching, and pushing each other around. The worst part was when they all yelled out "Marianne!" when we walked in, like we were on some twisted version of that old TV show *Cheers.* The smell of beer, boys, and piss smacked me in the face. The nausea rose in my throat like a song. I didn't want to think of how they all knew her name.

"'Ello, boys!"

I was grateful they went back to jostling each other instead of us. M sashayed up to one of the kegs and bent to pour some beer into her hand. She might as well've tied a leash around my neck the way I followed her. Bringing her hand up to my lips, I slurped the half-flat brew out of it and had to stop myself from licking up the rest. One of the Neanderthals sidled up to us and nudged my arm, pressing the rest of his drunk self up against my side.

"Wanna do a keg stand? Dude, your friend here did like five or eight last night."

Wow. I'm surprised you can count that high, dude.

I shook my head, wiping my lips with my sleeve. What I wouldn't have given for Blockhead to be here now. At least he was a vaguely familiar ignoramus and knew not to touch me. I pushed dude back with my shoulder and stood at M's other side.

"We're not here for the booze, silly," M cooed, reaching up and pinching his cheek like he was a naughty little boy. "Where's that stuff you been promising? A bet's a bet—I drank you all under the table last night."

These out-of-towners didn't know M could drink more than a Susquehanna River guppy and still walk a straight line. The dude frowned like he was embarrassed, but nodded and waved over another dude, that type of football player who looked awkward if he wasn't tackling something. Dude #26 (his jersey number or his IQ?) was so big, he had to bend down for the other dude to say something in his ear; then he handed something over. I barely even blinked twice before Marianne grabbed whatever it was, kissed the first dude on the cheek, and hooked her arm around my neck, half dragging me (although I didn't put up much of a fight) to the door. Mr. Peek-a-Boo stepped in front of us just as Marianne got her slender hand on the latch.

"Where d'ya think you're going, kittens?"

"We'll be right back—we're gonna go get some other chicks." M smiled, always quick with a lie, but he didn't look convinced. I stuck my forefinger into my mouth and tried to bite what was left of my nail into a point, just in case I had to start scratching my way out of there. "I just stopped by on my way to see how many y'all needed. Your cheerleaders left before I did. I figured I'd go rustle up some of ours."

Mr. Peek-a-Boo sneered—his version of a smile, I guess—and opened the door for us. He slapped M's ass as she passed through, then mine, stopping me dead in my tracks. There were certain rules I lived by that pretty much kept anybody from getting hurt, especially me. One of them was that touching me required permission, unless it was M or someone in my family. I tolerated it sometimes, like the dude earlier. But if he'd tried to touch me again he would have gotten slugged, or at least my knee would have introduced itself to his groin, even though he was twice my size and hitting him might've meant my breaking a couple of fingers. Not to mention my possibly ending up in an unmarked grave somewhere in the woods. But dammit, if a girl couldn't adhere to her own rules, what would this world end up coming to?

I swung around, about to cock my fist into a punch, but Marianne caught me before I could deliver. She clamped her fingers around my fist and squeezed. I could hear her breathe, heavy and quick, on my ear.

"Hold on, love," she whispered. "You and me gotta get out of here in one piece." She backed me up to the car.

Mr. Peek-a-Boo sneered again. "Yeah, I like that one—ain't too foxy, but got a little piss in 'er. We don't usually get black girls. You got some more like her? Spice things up a bit."

If only I could have projectile vomited on cue. M opened the door and pushed me in. She ran around the car, jumped into the driver's seat, and peeled out of there, blowing a kiss.

Sliding around in the pleather bucket seats, not holding on to anything, my eyes closed. Marianne was taking corners like they were candy. Opening one eye just enough to see fuzzily through my eyelashes, I could see she was driving with her knees, both hands fumbling around in her purse for something. I shut my eyes tight and just let it all take me.

❧ ❧ ❧

"Opal, honey, wake up," M cooed as she jerked the car/truck to a stop.

The very bane of my existence has always been my name. My mother, Chanteuse, the "lounge singer" (more of a karaoke regular), had thought it'd be cute to name a dark brown girl after the milkiest white gemstone possible. She had a habit of naming things badly—herself included. I apparently never answered to Opal even as a baby, but Mama wasn't around enough to find me a suitable nickname. Gran thought my name reminded her of "back home"—somewhere in Virginia. Gran never went "back home," but she'd talk sometimes like she was still there. Of course, she'd only lived there for her first four years before her folks moved up here to find better times in the

North. Pennsylvania, with its coal mines and steel factories, was about as far north as they could afford. Anyway, Mama and Gran couldn't keep calling me Opal, since I wouldn't answer when they called. So I was just known as Little Girl around the house until I got to school and Gran told me I'd better start answering to my given name, or else they'd just call me That Black Girl or worse. Most folks, if they called me anything, just called me O. I'm not telling if Marianne was M before I was O or vice versa. M, Gran, and Mama were the only ones who called me by my whole name anymore and usually only when they wanted to annoy me or really get my attention.

"Who's sleepin'?" I growled without opening my eyes.

I had a visualization of where we were in my head—parked in front of Kourtney Williams's house, the official cheerleader romper room. I pictured all of them sitting inside the cozy, country-style dining room, talking about everything they hadn't eaten in the past two weeks. I imagined Kourtney, the cheerleading captain, still wearing the tiny polyester black and white costume she'd worn before, during, and after the game, rapping her dainty white knuckles on the Pledge-polished, colonial-style oak table, asking the other girls to vote on whether or not they would accept our proposal to give it up to the rival team and hopefully spark some fire under the home team's unmotivated asses. Not just for free beer, mind you, but a call to arms, if you will. I had no desire to open my eyes onto that scene.

"C'mon," M said, pulling my coat. "Let's go have some fun, just you and me."

Now *that* opened my eyes. Surprisingly enough, we were nowhere near Kourtney and her band of cheerful raccoon angels. We were parked off Winters Road—I could tell by the distant sound of rushing water that we'd crossed the bridge at the ravine. Winters Road was hardly used anymore, just like almost everything else around here. Once the coal mines shut down, most people moved away to Pittsburgh, Philadelphia, or Harrisburg to look for jobs. Now there were just old boarded-up houses where most of the miners used to stay. We were almost equidistant from my house and town, give or take three or five miles, if you walked through some fields and woods on either side after crossing the bridge, but far enough by car so nobody, except maybe some mid-week campers or hunters, might see us.

"That's right, cool girl. Up and at 'em."

I got out the El Camino and followed M into the woods. Cold as it was, there were still some suicide leaves hanging from the half-naked trees. It was my favorite kind of day—steel gray skies, the brassy leaves on the ground giving everything an eerie upside-down glow. Marianne, ahead of me, was kicking up leaves as she walked, whistling a little tune to herself, just like she did way back when . . . back before things started tumbling headfirst downhill. Back before I'd started feeling like every moment she granted me was a precious flame in my hands—too hot to hold, too beautiful to let go. I gasped some cold air into my lungs to hold it, to remind me to forget.

"Race!" Marianne trotted back, tapped my forehead, then ran full speed ahead, flashing a smile back at me.

I chased after, scrambling through golden grasses, hopping from red-leaved bushes to brown-leaved trees, clomping through various depths of mud and muck. Laughing and screaming, we finally broke out of the woods into a huge meadow, the stiff yellow grass up to our waists. She collapsed, pulling me down beside her, and we panted in unison like puppies. What I wouldn't have given to stay like that forever—the dry, whistling grass towering protectively around us, just us.

"You old slug," Marianne teased, poking me in the belly, turning her finger into my layers of clothes like a screw. "You got more blubber than an Eskimo. But then, I guess you gotta keep warm in that igloo of yours." She put her fist over my heart, knocked on it twice.

I grabbed her hand, lacing her fingers with mine. Now, I could honestly say I wasn't fat, but she was surely skinny. Her bones were jutting out of her clothes more and more these days. Even though it was a little scary, I couldn't say I hadn't thought about running my teeth along all those ridges. She sat up, propping herself on one elbow, and grabbed my cap off my head, putting it backwards on her own.

Yet another rule I had that only M was allowed, or even dared, to break: no touching of The Hat. It was one of the few things I had to keep me close to my Pops, and it hadn't been washed since he'd last worn it some umpteen years before when he put it on my head. I only took it off to shower (even though I wore it swimming at the quarry) and almost always wore it to sleep. Mama and Gran were always pleading with me to take it off. When I was younger and they'd tried to dress me like a pink-ruffle-and-tulle freak show to ooh and ahh over, the only way I wouldn't hide under the shed out back was if they let me wear The Hat.

Back then it sat over my ears and most of my face, just the way I liked it. Now that M had it sitting backwards on her head, I saw how grubby it was.

"Baby, this thing stinks," she said, wrinkling her nose and throwing The Hat a few feet away. I got up to rescue it, parting the tall weeds and dry, whispery grasses that brushed up against my chest as I walked. I crouched down to pick up the hat and looked up at the gray flannel sky pressing down as the whispering stalks waved tall above me. It made me smile, remembering M and me crashing through a field like this (or was it this same field?) when we were little. We had been out looking for the slave-woman spirit who had flown through these parts so long ago. Gran and Mama had told us about her as bedtime stories. Just the thing every kid wanted to fall asleep to, right? I wondered if any of those stories were real or just made up. I wondered what that ghost would think of us now. As I started back, I saw something familiar to pocket.

"So's this the ride you promised me?" I asked as I sat beside her again, trying to sound as if I wasn't impressed. "I still got Gran's laundry to finish." Instantly I wished I'd just kept my mouth shut.

"Whatever, *Little Girl.*" Marianne cut her brown

15

eyes at me and flipped her tangled, frizzy hair that was the same spectrum of colors as any handful of autumn leaves—her hair was the most "ethnic" thing about her. Her skin was a pale gold. "If it was another era," Gran used to whisper, thinking we couldn't hear, "that child would've easily passed for white." M's hair was all kinks and curls, though. Gran hadn't known what to do with it when M was little, and when she tried to process it, it just got less kinky and more frizzy. It had at least six different textures that refused to be tamed—or at least, nowadays, M refused to tame them.

"I got a present for me and you . . ." She pulled a little plastic bag half filled with brown powder out of her pocket, along with a copy of *Moby Dick*. The book was mine—we'd read it for English class last year and I let M have my copy to study, but she didn't pass. In fact, I didn't even remember her showing up for the test.

"What, you gonna sprinkle some fairy dust over me to turn me into a whale?"

She gave me an exasperated look and thrust the book into my hand.

"Hold this."

Using a key from the glittery M keychain I'd stolen from the rest-stop gift shop on Route 80 when we were thirteen, she scooped some of the powder and tapped it out onto the book, drawing it into a line.

"What the . . ." I jostled the book and she grabbed my hands to steady it.

"Keep still. It's heroin. We're gonna try it."

So this was what she'd been up to lately. She'd been MIA from Woodrow Abraham Rootbaum High School (yes, we went to WAR High School; our own mascot, Woody Raccoon, was often used for target practice) for a long while. Until she decided to be on the Homecoming Court, that is. Then she started coming to look good on record, but she mostly just roamed the halls, carrying a fake pass she'd sweet-talked some teacher out of. It was like she was doing a guest-star appearance on a TV show—she'd wave and smile at everyone, wearing a wife-beater she'd sloppily written "VOTE FOR ME!" on in permanent marker. I'd heard the administration drew the line when she tried to Rollerblade through the whole school wearing a bikini and body paint.

Meanwhile, I'd been stuck taking a micro-computer technology class at the Penn State campus near Punxsutawney (go ahead, insert your favorite Groundhog Day joke). Gran was forever enrolling me in these things, especially since sophomore year, when my guidance counselor had actually called to recommend them so I'd "remain challenged" because I'd seemed "distracted." Since then, I always missed out on everything, especially M and her antics. I'd even heard that M had gone around flashing her boobs to all the after-school academic clubs, just to get their votes. Yeah, it was a real hoot to hear that news from the Science Squad.

M was as smart as anybody else (including me), but bored stiff by our town and high school—it was like living in a straitjacket sometimes. I kept going to school only because it was something to do instead of getting "a real job." Gran threatened to make me go work at the chemical treatment plant if I quit school. I could've graduated last summer but I didn't want to leave home without figuring out a way to take M with me. So, I guess M had found something else for entertainment. Not that I was a straight-edge or anything—I'd smoked herb a few times, drank, but it never really did much for me. And this? Snorting heroin—I didn't know if I wanted to watch this happen.

"I . . . don't think . . . I'm not really interested, M." I wrinkled my nose as she pushed the book up to my face. *How do I make her stop?*

"Aww, c'mon, Little Girl. Don't think. Live a little," she said. "I'll show you—it's not difficult or anything." She put her face down to the book, held her right nostril, and snorted the powder into her left. She raised her head, eyes closed, and smiled—the usual druggy-trance look you saw on every after-school special and drug-prevention video there was. I never thought I'd say it, but she actually looked pathetic.

While M was busy scooping out some more onto the book, I had this image in my head of Gran wandering around the yard in her housecoat and pink curlers, wondering where the hell I was with her underwear. The vision changed to her chasing me out of the house, throwing the curlers at me, when I came home with a drugged-out look on my face. And no laundry. When M raised the book to my face again, I leaned back, away from her.

"I'm gonna be in trouble with Gran already for being so late. You know how she is."

Marianne rolled her eyes at me, snorted the rest, then dipped some more out and did it all over again. Finally, she licked her finger, wiped the remaining residue off the cover of the book, and stuck her finger into her mouth. Shoving the thick book back into her pocket, she reclined on the flattened grass with her eyes closed. Looking down at her, I thought about all the things I wanted to tell her, about my Escape Plan to get us out of here come springtime if she could just chill. If I got scholarships to the schools I'd applied to, we'd be set and I could take her the hell out of here. For almost a year now I'd been scheming how to convince her that we could live together and I could take care of us and go to school. But I couldn't bring myself to say anything—not while she was like this. I pulled the present I'd found for her from my pocket and laid it on her chest.

Opening one eye, she squealed, "Wishes!"

Asclepias syriaca—known as milkweed (you knew you were an official nerd when you memorized scientific names of common weeds). Its teardrop-shaped pods held about fifty little seeds attached to those feathery white puffs you could see floating on the wind sometimes. When we were kids we just called them wishes. But in the natural world, those wishes carried seeds like parachutes looking for someplace to root. Back in the day, we'd catch those little white puffballs in the air whenever we'd see them floating by, making wishes on them with all our might. I always had the same wish.

M took the rough, ugly pod and cracked it open with her thumbnails. She pulled out the clean, silky strands and stroked them between her thumb and forefinger as the brown papery seeds fell neatly into her palm. One of the little wishes tumbled out and got stuck in her hair. I thought about picking it out and making a wish on it, a wish that would make her stay with me like this forever, but a gust of wind fluffed the milkweed out into a pretty little star and carried it off, away from me.

"So soft . . ."

I wondered if she'd fallen asleep—she had stopped talking and her eyes were closed—but after a minute she was rubbing the milkweed strands between her thumb and forefinger again.

"Hey," she drawled out slowly, like she was talking from a long way away. "You remember that ghost your gran used to tell us about? The woman who flew over the ravine—"

"Yeah! I was thinking of her just a minute ago."

"You were?" She opened one eye. "Did you see her?"

"See her?" I almost laughed out loud.

"Yeah," she said, dead serious. She opened the other eye, too, kind of challenging me. I said nothing so she'd continue. "More than once. Sometimes I come out here, you know. Just to look down that ravine and wonder what it was like . . . to fly like that, over the ravine and away from the past. Away and safe, you know? I loved that part—I can barely remember the rest of the story . . . But when I see her she's usually just standing there on the other side of the ravine. I saw her last night, too . . . when I was with Brock . . ."

I stayed quiet, held my breath, waited for her to finish. Her forehead wrinkled like she was confused, like the story got lost in her head.

"You know that jerk asked me to marry him?" She changed the subject, shutting her eyes again. "Like I was going to stay in this freakin' town and squirt out his babies while he goes to his little office or whatever it is lame jocks do after high school!" Her upper lip curled in disgust. "I told him I wouldn't wish that shit on anyone . . ."

I lay down next to her, wanting to know more about her seeing the ghost.

"I used to have so many wishes . . ." She laughed a little, but in a sad way, and was quiet again. "Mostly just to get out of this town, go to Hollywood . . . And only come back when I was a big star . . ." She laughed without any humor.

She suddenly grabbed me, hugging me. I didn't know if it was the drugs or what.

"You'll still think of me after you figure out the

cure for cancer or build a rocket or whatever it is your gran's got you going to college for, right?" she asked. Her body was clamped around me and for a minute I couldn't hear anything but the thumping in my chest.

"Think of you? I'm never leaving you," I said, wanting to say more.

She shook her head and laughed. "I always swore to never let you waste your life on me, girl, no matter what . . . You got better things to do."

What she said broke my heart, making me want to spill my guts about everything—she seemed so lost. Maybe a little idea of hope to let her know I had an almost concrete plan of how to make her wishes come true. But I couldn't, not until I knew for sure, just in case things fell through with Stanford. Gran really wanted me to go to MIT for quantum physics; my grades and scores were good enough so I applied, just to see if I could get in, but I didn't think M would move to Boston so easily. Maybe to New York if I got into NYU, but all she'd have to hear about Stanford was that it was in the same state as LA and she'd have her little pink suitcase packed. It had always been her wish to be a "LA-LA girl" (as she was known to say), and I'd been working my butt off for years just so I could be the one to make it come true. I didn't really care what I studied or even where I went to school—just so long as I could be the one to fly M out of here. But I couldn't let the cat out of the bag yet. What if I didn't get in? Or what if I didn't get a scholarship and couldn't afford to go or get us an apartment? There were too many ifs right now. Gran was always telling me not to worry about stuff like that, but I didn't think there was any way for the family to whip up that kind of dough. I'd kill myself before I'd disappoint Marianne again. Besides, I'd know for sure any day now. There was plenty of time.

Marianne was in my arms and I held her gratefully, trying not to hold on too desperately. It'd been a long time, seemed like forever, since we'd been alone together like this, since we'd been our true selves. The last time was more than a year ago in our secret place under the blackberry bush . . .

M shuddered in my arms like she was freezing cold. Her being like this scared the hell out of me. If I could just get her to come home with me, Gran could knock some sense into her, make her remember who it was she belonged to.

"This time I told that ghost to fuck off," she

whispered into my neck, her lips brushing against my skin. "She just stood there . . . like she could see . . . everything. Like she was judging me . . . like she knew me . . ."

Marianne pulled away and looked into my face; her eyes were all puffy, but still kind of unfocused and soft. Those eyes I'd searched a thousand times before, searching for a hint of the same kind of feeling that was burning me up inside.

"Nobody knows anything about what it's been like for me." Her tone changed bitterly.

"What're you talking about? I know—I was there, Mlapo. I'm Omali—I get you."

"Omali? Mlapo? You've got to be kidding me. That was so long ago!"

I could almost see down her throat as she laughed.

"None of that matters now!" Spittle flew out of her mouth. "You think you get me, but you have no idea!"

She wobbled to her feet, looked down at me, and laughed. She laughed like she knew everything that was in my head and couldn't give a damn. "You don't get me!" she said, almost losing her balance. That laugh of hers cut at me like a ten-inch serrated-edge hunting knife (complete with its own bottle opener). "Nobody gets me," she shouted. "Not even me!"

She turned and trotted away. I got up to follow, but I paused. The thought of running after her suddenly made me tired, like I had lead weights tied to my heart. She cartwheeled and finished with a perfect round-off, doing another down the hill. The golden grass was almost as high as her golden head now—all of it looked on fire with the sudden break of autumn orange sun in the gray sky. It was so freaking beautiful, I realized I was holding my breath, holding the picture of the moment inside me. But she looked back, stopped and stood there, reaching her arms out to me. The old urge flared in me—I couldn't help but run toward her. *Maybe this time* . . . As I got close, M turned and bolted again, disappearing into the woods.

Two

The twinkling of M's homecoming tiara bounced off the broken shafts of sunlight ripping through the trees. By the time I couldn't see it anymore my longing had gone with her, and so had any hint of the sun. I still felt the same way, like she was the only thing in the world for me, but for some reason there was no puppy-dog desire to scamper after, just to have her pull away again. Standing there, having her run away from me for the thousandth time, there was something different—in me. I didn't want to chase her to wherever she was going right now; it seemed too fast and too far this time—I felt like my heart might explode trying to catch up.

I looked up at the sky, like there were supposed to be some answers there. Waiting for it to come down, trying to figure it out, this feeling. It rumbled in my heart, rolled over, and crashed on me like a wave.

I thought of the only time I'd ever been swimming in the ocean. Chanteuse had gotten it into her head once when M and I were about six or seven that the big sea was summoning her. She could've just taken us to Lake Erie, a couple of hours' drive away, but when Chanteuse got something in her head, it stuck. She talked about The Ocean like it was a magical creature who would grant us all our hopes and wishes, whisper salty answers into our questioning mouths.

"Once you swim in The Ocean, Little Girl, she gets into your veins and gives power to your blood. We're all gonna be changed."

M and I were excited until after we got on the bus; it was a long and boring ride and I got locked in the funked-up bathroom twice. When we finally arrived in New Jersey almost a day later, it was dark and we all sat huddled up on a bench on the boardwalk, waiting for the sun to rise. Mama hadn't thought of getting us a place to stay. In fact, she told us she planned to turn us around and take the next bus out of that little seaside town—after we'd become one with Mother Ocean, that is. It didn't seem so strange that we were the only people out. We watched the sun come up and Mama took us down to the water as the clouds started swallowing the sky. I was a tough kid, but I was nervous that close to something so huge and powerful; it was endless. We'd taken a couple of trips to Lake Erie in the summers, but this was very different. Waves were throwing themselves about like angry old men, their peaks a frothy, yellowed white. The smell of salt water and sand opened my sinuses, stung them. But at the same time, the smell was warm, a welcome.

The weather was cold and windy. Still, once the light broke, Mama had us strip down to the bathing suits we'd worn under our clothes and she began to dance on the pebbly shore. M was as excited as Mama and wove pieces of seaweed into her hair, calling herself a mermaid. My feet hurt from the sand that kept sticking between my toes, cutting the tender skin. I picked my way along the beach, picking up pretty stones that caught my attention. It wasn't so bad until Mama wanted us to get into the water. The waves were still fierce; I realized Mama was yelling to make herself heard over their wild protests and the whipping wind.

"We'll just go in a little. Then we'll truly be a part of the power of the natural world," Mama shouted close to our faces. M all but ran in; Mama had to practically drag me. She had both of us by the hand, two girls pulling her in two different directions. Almost as soon as we put our big toes in, the frigid waves swept us up and began tossing us about like we were their very own playthings. Water that was no higher than our knees at one moment was over our heads the next. We had just been standing there; then all of a sudden we were being yanked farther out by the force of the current, in water so cold it burned. I turned my face toward the shore, thinking I could make it back if I could just run, if the shore would stay still and stop moving away. Then I heard M let out a little yelp. Turning to find her, I had only a second to hold my breath as a wave pulled itself up into a wall of water above our heads. Mama tightened her grip on us and dove into it. I remembered when Pops used to throw me into the air, that flying/floating feeling that took my breath away; I pictured it in my head as the sea had its way with us. My daddy's face below me, him wearing that green cap, arms outstretched to catch me. Surfacing, I gasped for air, just in time to be hit by another wave. Mama was still gripping me, and when I came up, I saw she still had Marianne, too. Salt water burned in my throat and my eyes. Next thing I knew, we'd caught a wave that bestowed some kind of mercy on us and spit us out onto the sand. We were all coughing and spitting, trying to scramble farther ashore, trying to get away from the water that was still licking at our calves.

An officer and some paramedics were racing down the beach toward us. Apparently, someone had seen us go in and called for help. They were crowding around, checking us out, asking if we were hurt. But we were all just fine. The cop said Mama must have gotten some superhuman strength to pull us to shore like that. When they got us wrapped up in towels and blankets, they began looking at us funny, asking Mama why she'd taken us into the water—didn't she know there was a hurricane coming, that we all could have been killed?

"We stuck together, so we were bound to come out just fine, right, girls?" Mama said. "Besides, if the sea had wanted us, she would've taken us."

She asked them to drive us to the bus station, and even though the looks on their faces said they weren't sure if Mama was crazy, they took us there anyway. I think they were just happy to send us on our way. We got to ride in the back of the police car, and M sweet-talked them into turning on the sirens. We rode past all the houses and stores people were boarding up, preparing for the storm, the sirens wailing like lost children, M howling along with them. Mama sat there with her eyes closed, a big smile on her face. I just couldn't wait to get back home.

I came to my senses—still in the woods, no waves, no Mama. M was nowhere in sight. I thought I might've heard her singing "The Glamorous Life," but I couldn't tell for sure. That feeling inside, that heavy pain (Love? Jealousy? Hatred? Boredom? It all was beginning to feel the same), was still there. My first thought was to find M, but remembering Gran's underwear, I turned and headed back toward the leaf-littered road.

꿈 꿈 꿈

"Little Girl, somebody told me you went off and left my unmentionables down over at the Drip 'n' Drop and let yourself get whisked away by someone else who shall remain nameless. I know you better have my laundry."

I rolled my eyes. Like anybody would take that old woman's drawers. I'd just walked in the door after stowing my bike under the house. A huge pack of laundry was strapped to my back. And here she goes, poking her little old head around the doorway, yelling from the kitchen, trying to be heard over the simulated sex scenes of one of her soaps.

"I also want you to tell me why you tracking all this mud into my house like you got no sense. You just like your daddy."

I knew she was probably touching the locket she kept around her neck, just as she did whenever she talked about my father. Gran loved my Pops more than anything else in the world, so I knew she was mostly fussing because she was missing him. The locket had bits of his hair and my own inside it.

Though my Pops grew up in this town, the only thing he'd say about it was "I'd rather've grown up here than in any big city. If you'd see how our people live in them ghettos you'd know it's depressing. Sure, there ain't so many friendly faces, but at least here you got nature to rely on. And you can always see the stars."

Those were two of the most important things to Pops. The third was family. Pops was an independent trucker now; he used to drive a regular local route, but now he owned a rig and got jobs for himself, so he was always working hard all over the country to send money to us. We hadn't seen him in a few months now, but he'd promised to make it home for Thanksgiving. He was always good on his promises. It broke our hearts not having him around all the time. The only one who wasn't missing him so much was Chanteuse, who was barely ever here herself. Way, way back in the day, she'd tried for a while to go with him and sing at clubs and truck stops on his routes, but she had come back home after two weeks, saying she'd discovered that as much as she and Pops were in love, they felt it most when they were apart.

"I knew it after the seventh day, honey. There were reasons I agreed to marry a trucker, and not just to get out of working that tollbooth. Our love is like a bird and must always be free to fly. Besides, your daddy was getting on my nerves."

Mama and Pops were the two different-est people on earth, as far as I knew. Mama was always talking crazy, Pops hardly ever talked at all. That's why I loved him so much—we were so much alike. Not that I didn't love my mama—we got along fine when she was in and out periodically, doing karaoke gigs. If she came home for more than a few weeks, we'd start getting in each other's way. Gran said she saw us starting to melt away into oil and water—one of us icy cold and the other one slick, one having to give way to the other. Used to be that whenever Mama would come home, we'd sit up late and she'd tell me about the clubs she'd sung at and her plans to be a regular singer in a nice lounge somewhere, maybe even put out a CD. I enjoyed listening, and for a little while, I became her audience. Mama sewed new outfits for her popular numbers and sang for me. But after a while, it got old—she expected me to stay captivated and got all frustrated when I didn't. I knew exactly why she and Pops lived separate lives and loved it. Up until she and I reached that breaking point, she'd do stuff like make chocolate-chip pancakes in the middle of the night and wake me up to eat them while watching the dawn. Right now she was learning how to sing and play piano properly with a teacher in Pittsburgh, so she's out a lot, still trying. Always trying. That made me kind of proud.

When her show was over, Gran came down the hall to the linen closet where I was putting towels away.

"Any mail for me?" I asked, trying not to sound like I was expecting something.

Gran narrowed her eyes at me and ignored my question. "It's been over four hours since you and Little Miss So-and-So disappeared from the Drip 'n' Drop, my source informed me."

Her "source" was none other than Mr. Drip 'n' Drop himself, Roscoe Mullins. The Dripster, Drippy, or Drip, as I also liked to refer to him, was owner of the one and only laundromat in a fifteen-mile radius of our town, but he spent almost all of his days gossiping on the phone with Gran—they fancied themselves to be town spies. M asked me once if I thought they were still doing IT because they were always going to bingo games until very late at night and ol' Drippy had a big 1979 baby blue Cadillac Sedan DeVille. Every time the Dripster complained about needing new shocks, M and I curled up with gags and giggles. Sometimes, when he thought I wasn't looking, I'd see him pinch Gran's bottom as she bent to get into the car. She'd smack his hand away like he was a frisky puppy, but she still tittered like a freshly hatched chick on Easter day.

Way, way, way back in the day, the Drip used to be a "leader" in the community, the football star / war hero who married the prettiest girl in town, whose daddy was chief of police at the time. When his wife died about fifteen years ago, he and Gran "kept company" full time. But the Dripster had been coming round my house for much longer than that. In fact, most everybody knew, before I was even born, that his car could be seen in our drive many an evening.

I'm sure it'd been a scandal at one point, people wondering what a handsome, prominent white businessman, married to a respectable young lady, was doing with a poor, woodsy-looking black woman who was ten years older than him. Let's just say Gran must've had it going *on*, 'cause even now it was out in the open with Drippy's wife gone, everybody knew they were in some kind of love. What else could he want with her after all these years, folks in town wondered? I think to most of them it would've been understandable if it was just sex, but this was something different. I wondered about that, too. Just goes to show—it doesn't matter who you love, just so you love them right.

Sometimes I see them sitting on the porch swing, just looking into each other's eyes, like they are still trying to figure out how and why they'd gotten together. It was never a story I could get Gran to tell. I'm guessing there were some bitter years, not having him all to herself. Plus, she had come to this sorry excuse of a town from Pittsburgh, pregnant already with my daddy, just like my mama came here for the first time pregnant with me. Gran's real husband, my grandfather, had been killed in the Korean War. Once, M and I found a box in Gran's closet with a blurry picture of him, a burial flag, a Purple Heart, and a letter saying how he'd died saving a bunch of other people. Our house was on his family's land; they had owned and farmed it for generations. But it had just been sitting there for years till Gran came back to it after my grandfather died— he'd never had an interest in farming, I guess. I had to learn all this from my mama since I couldn't have gotten a word about it out of Gran or Pops. They'd just look all sad and say, "He was a good man," and that was it.

Town folks whispered that Gran followed Roscoe here to raise his child, but Pops doesn't look a thing like Dripster, who, by the way, still hasn't bought Gran a washer and dryer, making me the one to have to hike down and do wash at the Drip 'n' Drop, along with the other work I had to do there. They tell me it's helping me to "build character and learn responsibility." Let's just say I wouldn't go out of my way to claim Drippy as any kind of grandfather of mine, just on principle. Other than that I liked him fine.

"Long as Roscoe keeps your gran happy and contributes, he all right by me," Pops had told me when I had gotten in trouble for writing my name and M's under the back seat of Drip's Caddy. I was about seven, so to me, it had nothing to do with Drippy—it was just another place for me to write our names, so people would know we'd been there. But I knew

Pops had meant that if Drippy was okay by him, he'd better be okay by me, too.

"Little Girl, did you use my fabric softener on those towels? They certainly don't look like they were hung out on the line in the country sunshine."

We'd gotten cable TV only a few years ago, not just because we lived way back in the woods, but because Gran had always been afraid we were going to attract too many UFOs with a satellite dish. Now that we finally had regular cable, Gran was obsessed with television. She and Chanteuse argued about it—Mama didn't think it was healthy. Gran took every third word she heard from commercials and programs as God's Honest Truth. And lately she'd gotten all crazy about fabric softeners.

From where we were standing in our little shotgun ranch house, I could see over the top of Gran's head, through the ripped screen of the front door, to a sheet of gray winter's-a-comin' sky. Creeping up on the horizon, the clouds were towering blue-purple fists in the twilight. My clothes still stank from riding past the chemical plant outside of town; my mouth still tasted like I'd stuffed a handful of nickels into it. I put my hands on Gran's small shoulders and looked sincerely down into her cloudy old eyes.

"That's because they weren't."

She chuckled. "You're such a bad granddaughter."

I leaned down and kissed her cheek. "Yeah, but I'm also the only granddaughter you got. So you better start treating me right."

Gran giggled in a way that made me think of her as a little girl. Her hair was a bright shock of gray against her smooth black skin, but sometimes, when she laughed like that, I could see her the way she must have been—a fun, laughing girl who fell in love hard and fast. She was still beautiful, fierce, and full of spark. There was nobody like my Gran.

She swatted my behind as I moved past her back into the kitchen. "And no, there wasn't any mail for you, 'less you want my bills." Gran followed me down the hall. "I trust you and Little Miss So-and-So had a nice time?"

I turned down the television and opened the metallic green fridge that matched the rest of the kitchen's dated décor.

"Why you mad at M?" I didn't really want anything in the fridge. I stuck my face in there just so I didn't have to look at Gran and bust into tears and have her pry the ugly truth out of me.

"Little Miss Thing hasn't been by to see me in a month of Sundays and can't even tell me herself that she's Homecoming Queen. Acts like she wasn't raised by me most of her life, as if she would've gotten any real care outta you-know-who!"

I knew she was mad at M's mother, Mary. Gran'd been mad at Mary even before M was born, for some reason she wouldn't tell. Mary was known around town as, well, in others' words, not mine: "A Certified White Trash Whore." Not like everybody else wasn't a Certified White Trash something or other around here (we, of course, were thought to be lower than trash because we were black. Half the time, to the folks in town, we didn't even exist). But Mary supposedly got pregnant by one of my Pops's trucker friends. Gran was always volunteering to take care of M, because "that girl's daddy was just like my own son, too." But really, I don't know if anyone ever saw Pops's friend again, including Pops. M never mentioned him except to say that she figured whoever her father was, he must've been a real dog to leave her and her Mamm (the Amish way to say "mom") like that.

I think Gran mostly couldn't stand the thought of even a half-black girlchild growing up with just Mary and Mary's father, Jinx. Mary was all right, I guess, but she never found much to say to either Marianne or me. Everybody knew to stay out of Jinx's way. Something bad was always happening to him, which made him just as mean as he was ugly.

"Granddaddy wasn't allowed to see me in the nursery at the hospital," M had told me once. "The nurses said he was scaring all the babies. But he never did scare me. He's the only one could ever put me to sleep."

Even though Jinx never scared M and really did treat her like she was the best thing that ever happened to him, I'd always been scared to look him dead in the eye, even after his stroke took so much out of him.

Town legend had it that Jinx left the Amish down in Lancaster when Mary was a teenager. No one had ever heard him or her talk about Jinx's wife, and nobody had balls enough to ask. Gran said they probably just got tired of looking at his ugly mug. I don't know about any of that, and I'm no Nancy Drew, but sometimes I heard Mary and Jinx having arguments in a funny, throaty language. It wasn't until much later that I found out they were talking in "Amish Dutch" and that M spoke it, too—but just around them.

"Marianne told me to tell you hey, Gran," I lied as I pushed a jar of pickled beets way into the back, hoping they'd get lost there forever. "She's been busy with this homecoming stuff; I haven't seen her in a minute either." At least that part was true.

"Hrmph."

"Awww, c'mon, Gran. Don't be mad. She was just saying she couldn't wait for your sweet-potato pie at Thanksgiving."

"She comin' over here? Oh Lord, that means I'm gonna have to get a whole turkey."

"Well, she said she'd probably just stop by for dessert." I didn't want to get her hopes up too high. But Gran had already turned the TV volume back up and gotten her grocery list out, mumbling plans of how she was going to make a huge gala feast for Marianne.

I made myself a tuna sandwich—the main staple of my existence—and headed off to my room. I promised myself not to think about Marianne.

There was a lot of time that passed as I stared out of my window, especially when that deeply bruised patch of sky rolled itself completely over to black, time I spent repeating my promise to myself not to think about M. Obviously I was lousy at keeping promises. It was one thing for her not to hang with me; I'd almost gotten used to our brief, superficial chats in the halls at school. But not to visit Gran, not even to say hi and get something to eat? That wasn't like her. She usually stopped by to chat with Gran and fill her belly. I wondered if I should be worried. Ha. That's a real knee slapper. When was I ever not worried about M?

The first memory I had of her was worry. Gran had always been talking about "that poor child" in whispers, and when I realized she was talking about Marianne, I wondered what was wrong with her. I knew her Mamm was never really around, but mine wasn't either. I thought maybe she was fragile like the dolls I always managed to pull the heads off of, so I was extra gentle with her and let her have anything of mine she wanted, until Gran got mad at me for letting Marianne wear my best (and most hated) dress out to play some magical fairy game in the woods. Don't think I ever really got used to saying no to M.

Here I was, thinking about her. Said I wasn't going to think about her again today. Wasn't going to think about her arms, stretched out to me. Wasn't going to think about her running away from me into the woods. And I certainly wasn't going to think about why I didn't run after her, tackle her, tell her I loved her, missed her. Why I could never get up the courage to . . . to do anything, really. I wasn't going to think about that. All blubber and no backbone.

My thoughts went to the same fantasy I always had of what it'd be like when I told everyone I was going to college on a full scholarship. Gran, of course, would cry, and Chanteuse would come home only after telling every tollbooth operator in Pennsylvania that her daughter was going to study at Stanford on a full ride. Pops would take care of telling everyone else on the way home from wherever he was. But to me, he'd probably just say, "Good job," or something like that. But M would be stunned—she'd be so ecstatic once I told her how I planned on taking her with me that she'd leap into my arms and never let go. But I didn't entertain those thoughts for too long. I didn't want to get my own hopes up too high.

I drifted off still in my clothes, the drone of Gran's TV like a lullaby. I slept heavily with no dreams, with only the vision of M leaning over me and looking into my eyes, humming "The Glamorous Life." I didn't even hear the knock at the door when Gran came to tell me that Marianne was dead.

THREE

I SAT up when the bed shook from her sobbing. Confused, I turned to see Gran's face gleaming, her tears reflected in moonlight. That confused me the most, really. She was talking, but I could only think of how everything had cleared, after those bully clouds had robbed the sky all day. I could hear Gran's voice, but I had no understanding of what she was trying to say. Her words seemed impossible. I looked at the full moon that took up most of my window, bathing the entire room with silver.

"... found her down in the ravine."

I lay back down and closed my eyes, trying to return to the dull silence of sleep. What was all this craziness she was going on about? Why was she making so much noise? Who was that screaming? I

just wanted to get back to that dream I was having—
what was the song Marianne was singing? I wanted
to feel her over me again. I wanted . . .

"Little Girl! You hear what I'm trying to tell
you?"

No. NO. All I heard was noise, when the only
thing I wanted to hear was whatever Marianne was
humming. It was all noise. I covered my ears. Gran
tried to pull my hands away. All I heard was noise,
the blood rushing like all seven seas in my veins.
Noise, screaming—I was the one screaming. Just not
so anyone could hear.

❧ ❧ ❧

I didn't know how long I stayed like that, my ears
covered to the noise, the insanity. There was no return
to sleep, though. Only my eyes clenched like fists.
Gran kept trying to come in, but I wouldn't listen,
wouldn't look. There was nothing to see, to hear. If
I just kept counting, miscounting the dots and swirls
behind the blackness of my eyelids, if I could keep
seeing Marianne's face there, looking at me, only at
me. If I could keep that, nothing else in the world
needed to be true. I found myself falling in and out
of memories.

There once was a time in my life when I didn't know that *night* was a mysterious word. I didn't know that it held terror for some people, that for some it meant sirens and gunshots and forbidden places. M and I had lived in the forest as if we were a part of it. Just about every day we had climbed and played in trees and knew the world from that perspective—upside down and high above it. In the forest we were warrior goddesses. The only mystery we knew was what we conjured in our heads. Gran was the only one who could yank us out of our universe and back into hers—not that it wasn't equally magical, but we had limited powers there. Those worlds blended together seamlessly, like those summers we spent lying under the blackberry bushes, turning ourselves purple. The overgrown blackberry hedge at the far end of the woods behind our house was our castle. Sometimes we'd just lie there all day, eating the berries until they made us sick with sweet. We found a little archway among its thorns where we could crawl through to a good-sized clearing. The sun crept in enough to make a fine carpet of soft moss. When we first discovered it, we were small enough to stand up in our castle undetected by any trespassers trying to make us come into the house to take baths. M hated when Gran would wash her purple off. "I'm the darkest berry!" she'd cry.

Once the house was quiet and the outside was alive with its own dark beauty, we joined the nighttime adventure. The forest had a different life in the darkness, just as we did. M turned into her true self—Mlapo, the brave, shimmering priestess of the heavens. I became Omali, mountain-raising warrior goddess of the earth.

We knew our land by heart. Once we crossed the creek and the place where we performed all of our secret ritual dances, Mlapo and I were led by moonbeams to where we hid all our most favored treasures. After climbing up the gigantic oak tree, we sat on its biggest bough, the one that had our symbol carved into it: *M+O 4EVR* enclosed in a heart. We'd carved it with the same knife we'd slit our thumbs with to mingle our blood. I reached around the far side of the tree and carefully withdrew a box from a crevice in the trunk. Mlapo opened it, revealing the tiny red feather that had once fallen from the sky and landed, without effort, in my outstretched hand. She also pulled out an arrowhead we'd found in the forest and some shells from our one trip to the ocean. Those were our most precious treasures.

When we emerged from the forest, exhausted by our journey, Gran would be sitting on the back porch in her favorite rocking chair, wrapped in heavy quilts and afghans she'd crocheted herself. M and I climbed the stairs, our eyes barely open, into Gran's open arms. In the morning, we woke again in our bed, as if we'd never left it.

Sometimes we made weapons of sticks, feathers, and stones; we'd fight each other in preparation of fighting with others—magical creatures, and sometimes the boys who thought they could go traipsing around our land. We sure gave them a run for their money. We planted booby traps and had secret lookout stations in the trees. One day, Mama got an angry phone call about us—we'd caught one of those boys up in our net and made him dangle for nearly three hours before we let him down, so his mother called our house to holler. Mama chuckled and told her we were Amazon princesses.

"What's 'Amazon'?" we asked as she hung up the phone.

"The Amazons were warrior women in Africa, my loves," Mama replied. She was in for some visit, wearing a veil and jingling, shiny bracelets that haloed her brown wrists. She was a traveling fortuneteller back then.

"Like in that story about Hannah?" She was our favorite.

Mama cradled Marianne and me in her arms, as she always did when storytelling. Sometimes she'd even draw pictures in the air with her fingers. M and I would watch in awe and wonder, seeing the story unfold like a movie. Mama read us books about African queens and goddesses, too; those stories would melt into the ones she'd tell about the people she knew and encountered in her life in different cities. Mama had friends and sisters and cousins all around the country who she would stay with sometimes, and we knew their stories of heartache and triumph. We never even asked what was real and what wasn't.

"Sure, my darlings. That's where Hannah's mother came from."

"That must be how she flew over the ravine!" We cheered in unison. That was the ending we were always told—those dirty slavers tried to catch her, but she flew herself clean.

"You keep telling them all that mess and they gonna really believe it," Gran said, but winked at us at the same time. M and I nodded to each other, having already agreed that Hannah must've been some kind of magic.

"Old woman, don't get started on me," Mama said. "You're the one who started telling about that ghost in the first place."

"They should believe it because it's *better* than true," Gran huffed back at Mama. They always disagreed on which stories were true, which stories were almost true, and which were outright lies.

"Girls, listen to me—you don't always have to believe the teller to believe the tale," Mama continued, leaning in and whispering. As Mama spun out the story, we watched her bracelets dance, glittering even in the dingy kitchen light.

52

❧ ❧ ❧

The only thing she could remember of her parents was being wrenched away from them. Somebody once told her that her mama was an Amazon priestess straight out of Libya and her daddy was a well-known king from deep in the tangled heart of Africa. It was a beautiful story, but she never knew if it was true.

They called her Hannah when she was bought to be a slave at a plantation big enough to satisfy all its own needs. An old woman called Whisper cared for all the children. Whisper got her name after her sons were sold from her—when she couldn't find solace for her grief, Old Master beat her silent, and she stopped speaking to anyone but the little children. She showed them how to work the earth in the vegetable and herb garden she was made to keep alongside Old Master's six-pillared mansion.

Old Master watched them from the porch some days, always wanting to see how much the children could pick, how much they could carry, which were weak, and which were strong. When they were able to pick enough tomatoes and okra for Old Master's approval, the children were ready for the tobacco fields. Outside the gated garden, Old Master's sons, Jameson and Rupert, were fat and idle. Hannah and the other children in the garden never got to eat the food they picked, unless they could do it without being seen. Up inside the big house, Hannah could sometimes hear the voices of two women. One voice sang sad, beautiful spirituals all through the day, and the other asked for more. Hannah learned that the voices belonged to Mistress, an invalid, and Alyce, the chambermaid, who was never allowed to leave the room unless it was to do or get something for Mistress. Alyce slept on the floor next to Mistress, who adored hearing Alyce's sweet, high voice, especially through her many sleepless nights. Now and then Hannah could see Alyce's sallow brown face watching her and the other children from the window. Hannah never saw Alyce leave the house.

Whisper taught the children to work, but she also taught them to think. She'd say rhymes to teach them facts, spell the names of the vegetables, and use any objects for adding, subtracting, and multiplying—all just under her breath, all under Old Master's sight. At night, she'd whisper names of the stars and sing quiet lullabies about Freedom.

When it was Hannah's turn to leave Whisper's garden, she quickly found out that everyone she worked with was thinking about Freedom, too. It was in every heaving breath, every drop of sweat, every ache and pain, every bend and pluck. All day, every day. While some thought about Freedom as something to go and *get, others thought of it as something to wait and receive. Either way, Freedom was on their minds. It was the only thing Hannah could think of while she worked all day, picking worms and beetles off Old Master's precious tobacco plants.*

After some long years of drudgery in Old Master's fields, Hannah was told early one morning to go work in the big-house kitchen. Cook had been caught sneaking over to another plantation to see her pregnant sister. When she was found, the dogs tore up her arm, so Hannah was sent to help her. Cook was made to wear a padlocked iron belt around her waist that connected all the way up her back to a locked collar around her neck. From there, an iron rod reached up like a thin arm into the air above her head, dangling a clanking cowbell just out of her reach.

Soon as Hannah got to the kitchen, a steamy building made of stone squatting behind the big house, Cook yelled over the clanging of the bell (it rang with every slight movement she made) for Hannah to fry up a steak for Old Master right away. Hannah had never been so close to quality meat before—it made her whole body ache with hunger. As she dreamed about what it might taste like, she accidentally let it burn a little on one side. Cook tried to help by covering it with potatoes and eggs.

Hannah carried the heaping, fragrant plate to the house, wishing for that weight to be in her belly rather than in her hand. Stepping into the house, she sucked in her breath—it was like entering another world. She knew Old Master and Mistress lived differently, more comfortably, than she did in the slave quarters, but some of their comforts, like soft, embroidered chairs, made her feel like fainting into them. She'd never sat on anything but the ground or plain slats of wood. Books lined the walls; Hannah never knew about any book besides the Bible, which she saw in Old Master's hands on Sundays, but of course she wasn't allowed to touch it, much less read it. The delicacy and number of little objects about the rooms and the halls struck her dumb. Hannah finally knew what she'd been tending so much tobacco for—their trinkets, their books, and their cushions.

Hannah found "the big room with the big table," as Cook had directed her, but Old Master scowled and grumbled at her for taking so long in bringing his food. He hastily pushed the potatoes and eggs aside and cut right into the steak. When his knife stuck, he became enraged and knocked Hannah to the ground with his silver-knobbed cane. He would not tolerate burnt food—Old Master spit as he spoke—not at all. He looked down at Hannah for a moment, as if trying to fix her features in his head, and then went back to the table. Hannah got up as quickly as she could, holding her throbbing shoulder where he'd hit her, and fled to the kitchen while Old Master fed his dog the steak and gobbled down the potatoes and eggs himself.

Each time she went into that house ended up being painful. Old Master's sons, who weren't that much older than Hannah, insulted her every chance they got. If they weren't cursing her cooking—after the first time, she was fearful of overcooking and would often undercook the food—they were cursing her "wretched face." When Jameson and Rupert weren't insulting Hannah with their words, they were insulting her with their hands—grabbing and groping her body, trying to feel under her ragged, threadbare dress. It was a game for them to try to corner Hannah whenever she was in the house. Hannah was beaten for crying out, for disturbing Mistress.

One time, Alyce came down; Hannah barely heard her skirts rustle until Alyce was just behind Rupert, who was trying to force Hannah into a broom closet, telling her every awful thing he'd do to her once he got her in there. Rupert's whole hand covered Hannah's straining face; her fingernails gripped the door frame—she could feel the wood splintering. Alyce's voice was shrill as she told Rupert that his mother was asking to see him.

Rupert stomped off, disappointed he hadn't won his game. Alyce stood there with her eyes downcast and waited while Hannah caught her breath and fixed her torn sack of a dress. Hannah saw that Alyce was no more than a few years older than her, but small as if she'd shrunken inside of Mistress's hand-me-down dress. It struck Hannah as a bit frightening to see a black woman in a white woman's clothes. Alyce's features were soft and her skin had a pale shade over her natural clove complexion; Hannah couldn't help but think it made her look ghostly as she quietly stood there.

Alyce finally spoke up. "It's your struggle

they after. Don't fight so much. They be bored soon enough." Hannah couldn't think of anything to say; Alyce's words hit her just as hard as Old Master's cane. She stammered a reply, and Alyce nodded slightly before she went back upstairs, just as quietly as she had come down. For the rest of the day, Hannah got the chills each time she heard Alyce begin the same hymn Mistress had been requesting over and over since dawn: "See, Gentle Patience Smiles on Pain."

But as the months went by, Hannah never forgot about Freedom. She understood that all people suffer in their own way, but the world she lived in managed itself around pure insanity. It seemed as though she belonged to everyone but herself. Old Master read from the Bible and preached to all the slaves every Sunday from his porch about turning the other cheek, but most of his audience was scarred by his whip and cane.

Hannah wasn't sure she could stand it forever—she was already at the age for there to be talk about "breeding" her, Cook warned; she'd been forced to have three children in her youth with men she didn't even know. All of her children had been sold. One cool, starry night, on the kitchen porch *after dishes, Cook told Hannah her sad story while Hannah held the tongue of the bell contraption so they could talk in quiet voices. Cook didn't know where any of her children were—her sister was the only family she knew close by. Hannah didn't want children, not if they were to be taken away from her and made slaves. Hannah feared having feelings or attachments to anyone, even if she were allowed a choice about whom she'd want to be close to, much less to love. Love wasn't a word often spoken by the enslaved.*

Four

AFTER DAYS of memory-dreaming, I returned to my present self. How could I be living when the only thing I had ever lived for was dead? I couldn't see M's face anymore, couldn't hear any more noise. I opened my eyes, looked out the window. No more hard steel clouds; the sky was that irritatingly soft baby blue of early morning. Frost on the ground sparkled menacingly. I could see the outline of the not-so-distant mountains, hunched shoulders confined in a straitjacket of mist. Birds were twittering like I even cared. I hated everything, and everything hated me.

I stumbled into the hall, tears and sleep caked in my eyes. Hearing the scuffling of Gran getting up from her chair in the kitchen, I threw myself into the bathroom and locked the door. I turned on the water for the tub and my shower radio full blast, so I couldn't hear what she was saying. I gargled as loud as I could. Gran finally gave up, I guess at least satisfied I was okay if I was making so much noise. She probably heard me getting up at night to use the bathroom and saw I was pretty much sleepwalking. I settled into the bath and closed my eyes. The scent of Gran's eucalyptus and lavender herbs hanging from the ceiling of the pink-tiled bathroom began seeping warmth into my lungs and calm into my brain. The sadness leaked out of me in sweat and tears. This wasn't fair. Why was I still here, living? How could she be gone? But at the same time, I always knew that one day it would end like this. She'd always loved a tragedy. I wondered if she had been trying to take me with her. Or wanting me to save her.

Sinking down farther in the tub brought the water closer to my face, my chin, my lips. Pounding on my head with my fists, I tried to see her again, but the image wouldn't come to me. An insult to my injury— at the same time my brain couldn't stop thinking of her, it denied me the vision of her face. Maybe it was punishment for letting her go, for not chasing after her into the woods. This was all my fault, just like her not getting on the cheerleading squad was all my fault.

By tenth grade, M's plan to get people to forget she ever hung out with me had been kind of working. I mean, she'd had a fairly good chance for the squad, being more skilled at acrobatics than most of them. It had just been the social element that was threatening her chances. That was when Kourtney called me a dyke in front of the whole cafeteria, just to see how loyal M was. Well, let's just say things took a turn for the worse. After she cleaned up the mashed potatoes I dumped over her head, Kourtney told the varsity captain that she'd seen M and me making out in the locker room, which immediately got M kicked out of tryouts. It was a rumor I often secretly wished were true. Maybe if I had ignored Kourtney, just so M could've made the squad, maybe it would've been different and maybe she wouldn't have . . . Anyway, it was all my fault . . .

I pushed my own face below the surface of the water, holding my breath, making that delicate decision. Should I push the warmth of life out of my lungs, invite the cold in? There was the razor right by my hand . . .

"Little Girl? You too quiet in there . . . I'm coming in!"

I didn't think she actually had the key. She'd been hiding her set ever since M and I had hoarded all the keys in the house one cramped winter day, convinced one would unlock a magical gate into another world. Since we didn't know which one it was, we hid each of them separately to confuse the bad guys. Gran turned the whole house upside down looking for them and, after I finally admitted we had them, made sure we put everything back together in its rightful place. We couldn't remember where we'd stowed every one, but Gran somehow found them all. M and I were punished by having to sit with her and Drippy every afternoon for a whole week, listening to them bicker over *Divorce Court* decisions. Since then Gran had been keeping the keys hidden, but mostly from herself.

"Little Girl, don't make me come in there and yank you outta that tub!"

I heard her voice like it was in my own head. She was afraid of what I wanted to do, and she was going to do everything she could to make sure I didn't do it. I pulled myself up enough to see her standing in the doorway, leaning on the knob. Gran poked her little gray head into the steaming bathroom, her glasses immediately fogging up.

"I was about to try and bust down this door, but thank Saint Anthony I remembered where I put the key—inside my bra!" She grunted and tried to readjust herself back into it. Then, along with the tears and sweat, laughter poured out of me, too. I could imagine Gran taking a step back like she was going to ram the door, then digging all inside her bra instead. The absolute ridiculousness of everything in the world had just fallen on my big toe, but it couldn't fully distract me from the pain in my head, my heart. I was sobbing and shaking so much that Gran just sat on the toilet next to me, patting my head. She couldn't get me out of the tub.

"You remind me of when they found Hannah," Gran said after I quieted down some, my head and arms hung over the tub. "Lookin' all beat down after draggin' herself through that big hurricane. 'Member that part of the story?" I couldn't bring myself to even look up. "She was all weary like you are now when they found her. Holding on to that tree with all her might. Like it was the last ounce of self-respect she had. She was thinking it was them slavers trying to take her back, remember? She was expecting slavery, but it was a new life come to find her. Remember, Little Girl?"

She sounded like she was giving me a command rather than asking a question. I didn't want to remember anything but M, but Gran was going to tell the story whether I wanted to hear it or not.

Weeks after her encounter with Alyce, Hannah finally decided she couldn't wait for Freedom anymore. Alyce's life was not her own, but at least Hannah had privilege to simply leave the house, even if it was just to go to the kitchen or the storeroom. Although Alyce took care of another woman's body—bathed, medicated, soothed, and fed it—she could not claim that as hers, either. In that house of things, Hannah saw that Alyce was just another thing to comfort and amuse her owners. Hannah couldn't bear that for herself—it made her sick. She decided she'd do anything to get away, at least to try.

First Hannah got some advice from Cook, who told her she was a fool and she wouldn't make it, especially by herself—but she hoped real hard Hannah would. Then Hannah got some bread, a bit of dried meat, and a drinking gourd from Whisper, but no words. Hannah decided to leave after she helped serve supper, just as the light was turning. She had had no plans to leave that night until Jameson jabbed her backside with a fork while she was serving very hot soup, making

Hannah burn her arm as well as get slapped by Old Master for her clumsiness. Cook promised to cover for Hannah at breakfast and lunch the next day, so she figured she had until midday to get as far as she could and to find some shelter in which to hide during the daylight hours.

Cook believed some folks got all the way to Canada that way. She looked Hannah in the eye and said she would go with her if it wasn't for her sister, who was due any day. Cook drew Hannah a map in flour with her finger and showed her they were in Maryland. Across a great wide bay that led to the sea was the Delaware border. Cook said they wouldn't think to look for her there, if she made it across, that is. Hannah was surprised to realize how little she knew about where she lived. She had no idea where she'd be going, except "North." She'd heard stories of folks living for years in the swamps, never getting caught. Cook advised her to head northeast toward the Nanticoke River, that Hannah might find some Indians still there who might help her.

Cook also said she knew for a fact that Old Master was short on money—she'd heard him complaining to his sons about their mother's increasing doctor bills. He'd be reluctant to spend money on another slave catcher so soon after paying for Cook's return. But Cook warned that if they had to bring Hannah back, she'd surely be sold far south for hard labor to make up the difference. Hannah thought that after spending her life in slavery, she didn't want any more of it and would rather die than return.

Hannah remembered that thought on the third night as she pulled her cut-up, mud-crusted feet through the wet woods. She'd wrapped her feet in old flour sacks on the first night, but they'd fallen off and floated away with her other things. It was the season of big storms, after the heat of summer but before the leaves began to turn. It'd started raining not too long after Hannah set out—a good sign at first, since it'd be hard to find her footprints. But soon the storm winds were pushing against her like a wall. Hannah thought of Rupert pushing her into that broom closet, his palm digging a dent in her face. She reminded herself over and over that the weather was not her foe—it was washing away traces for them to find. If she could just go farther, she thought, just a little farther . . .

Hannah ended up just trying to stay afloat, even as she tried to make some kind of way northeast. She knew she didn't have much hope of finding anyone who'd help her. The day looked only two shades less gray than the night. When she could hardly struggle forward, she held on to trees, clung to shrubs. No matter how tired she was, Hannah hugged those trees hard because it felt good to hold on to something. She whispered prayers into them, asked them to keep her safe. The coarseness of their bark on her fingers, next to her face, gave her strength.

She was holding on to a big old oak tree with both her arms and legs when she felt someone trying to pry off her fingers. Hannah knew she couldn't fight back; she had barely enough strength to hold on. She was afraid to open her eyes and see Old Master's scowling face or, worse, the sneers of Jameson and Rupert. She groaned in agony when her fingers were finally loosened and flinched for the first blow. To her surprise, she was lifted up gently and with some care. Gathering her courage, Hannah opened her eyes onto a man like she'd never seen before in her life.

"Stop now, Gran," I cut in. "I can't hear no more." Those people were long, long gone. What did they know about what was happening to me? I'm sure they wouldn't have cared.

I held out my fingers to show her how they puckered in protest. Gran drained the tub and wrapped me in some towels, waiting patiently for my well of tears to dry. But the sound of the water making its final swirl down the drain was what really broke my heart. Down the drain. Everything down the drain. I got myself together after Gran had gone into the kitchen and I heard her on the phone, telling someone that she needed help with me. That brought some kind of sense into my head—Drippy coming over here with his Wednesday bow tie on, wearing that face . . . Couldn't bear the thought of him seeing me teary and naked, proud and possessed. I climbed out of the tub, still weak from the heat of the water. Gran's voice was all whispery, floating down the hall. Reaching for the sink, I thought I saw something in the mirror. The back of Marianne's head, her hair flying as she trotted out of my range of vision? Holding my breath, I leaned in closer, but it was only me and my green hat. My eyes were sunken and small. The skin around my mouth was ashy and there were salt tracks on the sides of my face. So much for cleaning up.

Standing there, staring at my own face for the first time in I don't know how long, I felt a numbness consuming my entire being. It started right at the center of my chest. I still couldn't see M's face in my head, and it was pissing me off. I didn't know who I was trying to impress, but I could feel myself hardening from the inside out. I couldn't see her face, but still she was haunting me. By not even showing up. No ghostly visions or feelings of her being present and trying to contact me from the other side. That's what I couldn't stand: alone.

When I finally got back to my bed, it hit me that for the first time in my life I couldn't just go and see her anymore, or run into her in the halls at school, not even to brush past her. This was the first death in my life. Shouldn't I have felt it in my heart when she died? I always thought when you were this close with somebody you'd feel or see something. Like in those "mysteries from the dead" shows Gran was always watching . . .

"You want to know what happened?" Gran asked quietly, watching me from a chair she had pulled up to the side of the bed. I did and didn't want to know. Wanted to keep it a secret from myself, but at the same time I needed to know everything. I nodded, covering my eyes.

"She fell at the ravine. Her neck was broke, they said. Probably didn't feel a thing, poor child. She must've been walking along and . . . slipped."

Pulling my hands away from my face, Gran focused her x-ray eyes on me, trying to get through. Little did she know—I was keeping everything about me shut tight.

"The funeral's today, Opal . . . You want to go?"

I knew for sure that I didn't. Gran had dragged me to a few funerals of her old lady friends. The thought of Mr. Nack, the town mortician, having his hands all over M made my own body jerk in revulsion. He'd make her up to look like a tanned Barbie doll in a display case. I couldn't stand that. And in church, where everyone would be shaking their heads and coughing into their handkerchiefs like any of their feelings mattered to the dead. The altar boys wearing dresses, looking at her, wondering what she felt like, wishing they'd had a turn.

"I just want to be alone," I croaked.

Gran always understood that and left the room quietly. Lying there for a long while, curled into myself as much as I could be. I could hear Gran on the phone again, talking in low tones. I didn't want to be gawked at. What I wanted was to get out of the house. Dressing quickly, I climbed out the window and grabbed my bike from where I always stowed it under the house, like I'd done so many times with M. Her bike was still under there, rotting away. Trying not to think, I flew through the woods to the road.

❧ ❧ ❧

I didn't begin to wonder about my strength until I could barely balance anymore. The roads around there were so small and winding, they made me dizzy. There were parts I had to walk. Walking felt like my feet were inside my head. The day was bright, blue, and crisp, but there were clouds fumbling over themselves to get here from the west. Maybe it was my head that made the clouds seem like they were moving at breakneck speed. Ended up cutting through three fields before I made it to the Flying Pan—town cafeteria extraordinaire. I fell onto a counter stool, where Gretchen, the old German woman who thought everything Asian was "adorable," was already pouring my coffee, having seen me come in. She was wearing a red satin embroidered dress with one of those Asian-style collars under her stained and greasy apron.

"I get you some eggs and potatoes, eh? You look like you need to eat."

She winked at me and patted my hand like it was going to make everything better. Just last week she'd ignored me for fifteen minutes before asking if I wanted anything to drink. I looked Gretch the Wretch in the eye, hoping she'd see every ounce of my loathing there.

"Don't you even say a word, hon."

I wasn't going to.

"I can't imagine the grief you must be going through."

Of course you can't, Gretchie, dear. You can't imagine anything I'm going through. Never have, never will.

"I was just saying to Charlie and the girls how *horrible* this must be for you and your family, too."

I had to remind myself just to stare into the black void of my coffee cup and wait until after I ate before spitting directly into this woman's face. Charlie was the cook. He was also one of M's Mamm's poker-party regulars, and Gretchen was foaming mad over that. She'd been trying to hook him and change him into a proper Christian for years. Although he spent most of his time with Gretchen, once a week he was knocking on Mary's door. M used to joke and say that her Mamm's Sunday night poker party was the only church that man would ever know.

The "girls" were all the rest of the old ladies in town. They spent most of their mornings at this dead little joint, mostly gossiping and spying on Drippy across the street. Every time I walked into the Flying Pan, all their conversations would stop. These gals still had their panties all in a bunch over Gran and Drippy, especially since most of their husbands had died and Drip was one of the only unmarried older men in town. They couldn't stand how the Dripster spent every waking moment he could either speaking to or being with Gran (I couldn't tell you why they didn't just live together now). But the ladies would still go over to the Drip 'n' Drop, all gussied up, lipstick bleeding into their wrinkled skin and their tightest housedresses on, just to "throw a few things in" the new ninety-pound washer while they had their breakfasts. Their lust for him was as thick and sticky as the grease on ol' Charlie's grill. The hate they had for Gran and the rest of us was addictive, just like the coffee they drank every morning. It got them going.

Usually I just grab my Flying Pan food to go, but today I was ravenously hungry and weak, and there was no place else to get something to eat in town—the nearest fast-food restaurant was a good fourteen miles away, right by the highway exit. I gobbled my eggs and potatoes without looking up. I could see that Gretchen was still standing there in front of me, although my hat blocked out her head and shoulders. She was rubbing her thumb across her fingers like there was something slick between them.

"She was such a lovely girl. What a shame."

Was this the same old bag who laughed so hard she snorted like a stuck pig when someone whispered loudly that M and I ought to be made to pick up our food at the back door?

The other women behind me were murmuring their agreement. I lowered my fork carefully. Maybe I was surrounded by aliens or clones—all the kindness was getting creepy. Alternate-Reality Gretchen leaned her hips heavily on the counter, speaking closer to my ear. "Did she leave you a note, *liebshien*? Hmmm? Say why she did it?"

And we're back, folks. How freakishly typical. I threw the couple of balled-up dollars from my pocket onto the counter and headed for the door. I stopped short, having a sudden and deep desire to set the record straight.

"It was an accident," I said, but my voice cracked in rage. "An accident!"

Rolling down the street again, I felt a little stronger. Or more like I felt madder. *No, Gretchen, my little strudel, she left me nothing. Not even the sight of her face in my own head. Nothing.* I began to feel that crushing numbness again, right in the middle of my heart. Next thing I knew I was headed for the ravine.

FIVE

ALL THE WAY THERE I could only think of her hands. The last time I saw her she kept reaching out to me. Chipped red nails, cutoff black gloves, fraying on the left thumb. Her lifeline was so *deep*, Mama used to say.

"If it got any deeper, you'd be able to see clean through it," she'd said, holding Marianne's hand up to block out the sun.

Marianne's hands were the reason we almost got kicked out of school for the first time. In third grade, no less. We'd lived our entire lives centered on ourselves and the world we'd made. Our first word was *us*. The only other people our age we knew were the boys we'd fought in the woods. Gran had homeschooled us, just as she did Pops, until they sent social workers out to check on us and said that although we tested higher than other kids our age, Gran just wasn't "educated enough" to teach us.

Real school had been terrifying on our first day. We had to ride the bus, and the noise and color of it consumed us—not to mention that we had to walk a mile to get to it. Instinctively, we held hands for protection and comfort. At first nobody seemed to mind. But then they tried to separate us, and all hell broke loose. For some reason that we couldn't understand, they wanted us in separate classrooms. I don't know what M did in hers, but I made a picture. The teacher wanted the class to paint pictures using our favorite colors, so I did. My colors were black and red, just like my feelings. And when I got finished, so was the floor and a good patch of the ceiling.

At lunchtime we were back together, clinging to each other like vines. The other kids were beginning to get nervous around us. I'm sure we looked like frightened little animals—they all looked like they wanted to poke us with sticks. Even the teachers were whispering and pointing. After lunch, we refused to let go of each other's hands again, so they called in the counselor. The counselor called Gran. Gran told them to leave us the hell alone until we got used to the damn place. We could hear her over the phone—she said that we were just close, and why was it such a big deal? Well, they told her, if we weren't mature enough to "work independently," we would be sent back to first grade.

When the counselor put us on the phone with Gran, she whispered, "If y'all don't give in to what this fool woman has to say, I'm gonna have to make y'all take lessons from Roscoe at the Laundromat."

Gran convinced them to leave us in the same class, but we weren't allowed to hold hands. School was hard in so many ways. M and I were already reading on our own—Mama and Gran had taught us—and we read to each other out loud. But it was painful to have to sit for hours in one room, listening to those teachers rattling off only a fraction of the things we'd already learned. We'd watch the other kids, unable to really enjoy whatever activity we were doing. The boys we'd fought hard with every summer since we could remember were now in class with us, staring and sneering. I found out early what it meant to punch a white boy. That caused enough trouble for me to keep my fists balled up but bolted to my sides or inside the pockets of my overalls. It was hard not to reach out and hold M's hand, not to let go of the rage.

The sky was completely gray again. The wind had picked itself up like an old man with a hernia, moaning as the half-naked trees rained leaves all around me. I rode face-first into it all, cursing Gretchen and her crew at the Flying Pan. They were like rubberneckers at a car crash. I hated them all.

I stood on the pedals and pumped my legs as hard as I could; our town was on a sorry excuse for a mountain—more like a hill that looked up to its sad big brothers. The Allegheny Mountains in Pennsylvania were the last creeping hands of the defeated monster known as the Appalachians. Pops had told me that our mountains were just little leftover sand piles from when the ocean was young and carried most of the land in her belly. My green hat, on the other hand, was from Vail, Colorado, in the Rocky Mountains. The Rockies were proud warriors, Pops had said. Took your breath away. Pops had traveled up, down, and across them in his truck. For a while, he had taken some jobs in Mexico and then Latin America. But he wanted to travel farther down through South America and see the Andes Mountains, said he would take me and Mama. Gran had said she didn't want to go rambling all over the world. Said she got too claustrophobic in the truck. Mama and Pops were the travelers. I never wanted to leave home . . .

Gran's story came back to me like a leaf on the wind—
Hannah leaving everything she knew to go trudging
through the forest, pushing herself to freedom. I tried to
remember what happened next, remember who Hannah
saw. I told the story to myself as I pumped the pedals of
my bike harder, fighting my way to the ravine.

≈ ≈ ≈

His skin was a rusted copper, his hair a dark forest,
long with thick waves curling. The bones in his face
looked carved right from the woods themselves; he
had a generous nose and soft-curving lips. His ears
were pierced, dangling a long, sharp animal tooth
on one side and a delicate shell on the other. He
wore a soft cotton shirt and purple and white beads
around his neck. He looked down at her, studied her
face, and smiled a little; Hannah winced trying to
smile back, her head hurting so. In her half-delirious
state she wondered what she looked like to this man
who was now holding her so close in his arms.

Hannah knew she couldn't sustain any
strength for long—just being held so tenderly
in his arms made her a little weak, and she could

barely manage to look fully into his bright green eyes. She turned her head a little and saw that there was another man, much older and lighter in complexion than the man holding her, but an Indian, too. The men talked in a complex language to each other that she could not understand. The older man placed a small pouch on Hannah's belly, telling her in perfect English that this young man was taking her to Delaware and that from there his people could show her how to travel farther north. Then, just as he told her the name of the man who was holding her so close, a gust of wind took the name away—all Hannah could hear was something like a piece of a song. She passed out before she could work her mouth to ask to hear it again.

When Hannah woke, she was lying next to a warm fire, wrapped in a blanket. The young man was trying to get her to drink a hot, bitter-smelling liquid. Hannah could barely lift her hand but managed to get a little down. After a while, she felt stronger and could drink some more. Finally she could sit up, propped against a big old birch tree. He reached into his sack, pulled out a pair of shoes like his own—they were handsome, handmade deerskin shoes—and handed them to

*her. She took them in her hands and turned them
over and over. They were beautiful but simple. The
leather was soft and sturdy. Hannah only knew
whites to wear shoes often—much less shoes made
of such fine, soft leather. She was so overcome
with feelings, she could only stare at them. She
knew she had nothing to give to anyone. She was
stealing her own self. The man shifted, making
her look at him. She tried to manage a thank-you,
but tears spilled out instead. She wanted to get
herself together, but the man, not understanding
her tears, gently pulled back the blanket to reveal*

*her freshly washed feet. It made her cry even more
with gratitude—she noticed, too, that he had
washed her hands and face of the days of mud she
had crawled through. He reached to help her put
the shoes on, but she couldn't let him. The thought
of watching him touch her was almost too much to
bear. She struggled to put them on her feet herself,
still trying not to look him in the face, but in the
end she had to let him do it—she was too weak.*

*She drank some more of the herbs he brewed
for her from the pouch the older man had given
her and slept deeply through the night. At dawn,
Hannah woke to the smell of something delicious.*

He'd caught a rabbit, and it was roasting over the fire. Hannah ate until she felt the strength to stand and finally to walk. They walked slowly and in silence for the entire day, stopping often for Hannah to rest. He led, keeping up a steady pace, holding back branches, and pointing out muddy spots to step around. The ground was soft with layers of leaves, and the trees swayed above them, moaning and shivering, showering them with dew. When the sun was high he reached into his bag and pulled out another pouch. He handed Hannah a piece of dried meat, took some for himself, and continued walking in silence. The next time he looked back at her, he smiled crookedly with the meat still dangling from his mouth. Hannah couldn't help smiling, too; she couldn't help liking him.

As they walked, Hannah thought of many things that caused her heart to ache. What would she do in the North? Where would she stay? She couldn't expect everyone to be generous in the cities, not from what she'd heard. She had no one, nothing. These thoughts made her feet and legs feel heavy; she nearly dropped to the ground when they stopped in a cave to rest late in the day. He brought her water from a stream, caught them a fish, and made the fire to cook it. Hannah felt miserable and useless, but he shook his head every time she tried to help. After they ate, she tried to think of something to say so he would understand her gratitude and forgive her tears and her weakness, but he suddenly spoke in English before she could.

He told her how his mother had been brought from Africa and that she, too, had escaped from her captors and was found by his father's people, the Nanticoke. She lived as one of them even after his father and his seven older brothers died defending their land when the state of Maryland declared war on them. Many lived this way, he said: African, but living as his father's people, following their traditions. It was rare, he said with a soft smile (or was that the firelight?) on his face, to see a woman flee on her own—especially to have gotten as far as Hannah did. He praised her courage, but in the same breath he told her how times were dangerous for anyone unfamiliar to the area to be traveling alone. There were folks robbing even freed blacks and Indians of themselves, he told her, kidnapping and selling them down south.

Hannah sucked in her breath, hearing that.

She was nowhere near safe. How far would she have to run? She couldn't hide the fear on her face, but he told her he would do everything he could to make sure she found safety. He promised it. Finally she looked into his eyes and saw she could trust him. She told him her story, how she decided to leave and why. Afterward, they sat there for a while, with the darkness falling heavily all around them and the fire sending sparks to the heavens, just looking at each other like they'd never seen another person before.

He woke her again after she'd slept a few hours, wrapped her in the suede blanket he'd covered her with during the night, and they began to walk. Although she was used to getting up in the darkness to help Cook with Old Master's breakfast, this was still night, as far as she could tell. When she stumbled, he took her arm and didn't let go. It was the first time she'd felt so completely at ease with him. But she still didn't know his name.

As the light of day stretched out around them, she asked what his name meant. He told her it had meaning only to his people—it was a name spoken in an ancient language that was quickly dying out. She asked him to say it again. He turned to her with a face full of hope. The word was like song rather than sound, and the wind again took it away before she could catch it and make it stay in her mouth.

Hannah's frustration showed. He touched her face softly.

"There are things," he said, "more important than names, than words." He told her he would answer to any name she chose for him.

"What would you like to call me, Brave One?" he asked, and gently touched her forehead with his.

Her brain buzzed from his touch. She breathed him in and thought for a moment. She blurted out her answer:

"Mine."

He kissed her there and then.

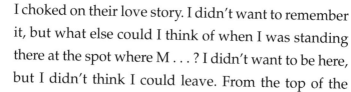

I choked on their love story. I didn't want to remember it, but what else could I think of when I was standing there at the spot where M . . . ? I didn't want to be here, but I didn't think I could leave. From the top of the ravine, which wasn't that deep, it seemed like the slope was manageable, but I knew it was rocky and easy to slip and get pulled down.

A little voice somewhere inside me said to throw myself down there—*what's left?* Looking down made me dizzy; I doubled over, feeling sick. *She kissed you first,* another little voice reminded me. I went down to my knees with that thought. It was true. M had wanted to kiss before I had even thought about putting my lips on anyone else's. It started with a game, of course. We were lying under the blackberry bush, seeing if we could pass the berries back and forth without our hands. It was all so sweet and innocent . . .

Don't think, I told myself. I looked down instead. Close to the water that was once a river, now no more than a creek, I could see where the police had set up their yellow ribbons. Like there was some crowd trying to mess up the crime scene. Cops around here were just itching to use that stuff up, trying as hard as they could to make everything they did seem important.

All along the lip of the ravine, trees and more trees were bowing respectfully over the edge, their roots buckling and twisting above ground and then plunging back again into the earth, leaving only a little space for walking. So I pulled myself up and walked toward it.

Edges are beautiful things—certain, sweet. The delirious, delicious rise of the belly, tempted with the first look down. The first step is the real shocker, only because the ground does not meet you with its usual defined compromise. But the rest, my friends—forgive the pun—is downhill from there. The second shock is how easy it is for your body to give in. The beautiful talent of flight is the ability to trust air just as much as you trust land. Any cartoon character can tell you that. Once you lose your trust in air, you find yourself falling . . .

No. No thinking. I wrapped my hands around a red spruce; the deep, rough grooves of its bark peeled back against the grip of my fingers and brought me back to earth—where the one thing I loved most was dead. What was it like for her down there, at the bottom of the ravine where the water bubbled and plucked out a tune? How long did she lie there alone? The yellow and black tape flashed in a sudden gust of wind. The trees littered the air with their leaves, precious castaways. My heart wanted to explode. Part of me wanted to only be feeling. Aching for her—like I always did. I'd give anything for that ache now.

The blackberry game changed so quickly into kissing, I think I just thought it was part of the game. But one day I realized I was more interested in kissing than in eating the berries. Those were the days when school and home were the dreams and our reality was under those bushes . . . It was everything to me, but maybe it was too much for her. She always wanted so badly for everyone to love her. But nobody loved her more than me . . .

Still holding on to the tree, I leaned over the edge of the ravine and held my other hand out, palm up. Closing my eyes, I wrapped both my hands around the hard, coarse texture of the spruce. Slipping from my own sweat, wanting to cut myself open.

If I could just live in memories of us . . . Like the time we'd convinced ourselves we saw Hannah. She was so real, we waved back. We'd gone out looking for her one day, and even when she was suddenly on our side of the ravine, we were only struck by her beauty. She wore a thick, yellowed shawl with some kind of Indian design; her dress was a simple brown, only a shade lighter than her skin. She seemed to be some kind of princess. We looked at each other, our jeans worn thin from playing so hard, dirt on our faces and in our hair. Both of us were wearing Dutch Wonderland T-shirts from the only trip M's Mamm ever took us on; we went for the wedding of a favorite cousin Mary grew up with in Lancaster. We begged and begged to go to the theme park on the way home.

Dutch Wonderland was a little amusement park smack in the middle of Amish country. Mary had worked there as a girl and still knew some of the ride handlers and counter girls. We got on only one ride, an old wooden one, and ended up sick from eating too many funnel cakes . . .

My hands on the tree again. This was what was real. My hands. The earth. Not a ghost or a memory. This ravine: filled with the very last presence of her. And me, stupid me, not even able to see her face. Not even in my own head. What a sad joke.

We had been wild girls and we knew it. Loved it. Gran, Chanteuse, even Mary, knew it and loved it, too. They reminded us with stories of themselves, their families, gods and goddesses—we never asked which was which. Pops would ride us around town and take us to the Flying Pan, calling us his "wild Indian princesses," each of us on one of his knees. High up above everybody else in his sparkling black monster rig that displayed a sign in purple on the grill: DADDY'S GIRL, with a bursting red heart in the middle that he didn't even have to say was for me. Then it all changed.

Tiny, evil voice in my head: *She was the first to leave you behind.*

"Little Girl!" A real voice behind me. I turned my face away from the ravine, opened my eyes. Yellow and brown. Brown and yellow. Hannah, flown back over the ravine, standing there. Just looking.

"Little Girl—don't you make me have a heart attack out here in these woods!" Gran, in her rubber duck boots, shaking her fist at me. The wind suddenly unwrapped the thick coil of her bun and her hair whipped about like a white fire above her head.

Hannah was gone.

Marianne was gone.

I was still here.

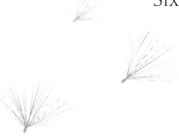

Six

In Drippy's Caddy. Baby blue everything. Lying on my back, sloshing around in the giant back seat. I imagined myself in a baby blue coffin, a runaway hearse. Gran had Johnny Mathis, one of her oldies favorites, blaring like it was gangsta rap. There were harps and some violins plucking away in the background, and Johnny was crooning: *"Chances are . . . "*

Trees raced past too quickly, making me nauseous so I shut my eyes, falling in and out of sleep. All the while, my fingers traced the place under the seat where I once penned our names inside a heart: *M+O 4EVR.* Johnny kept singing.

The car finally came to a full stop and Gran shifted into park. "Little Girl?" She put her hand on my shoulder. I opened my eyes, sat up. Of all the worst places, Gran had brought me to Wal-Fart. *Why must she subject me to additional agony?*

"Girl, you see what you needed to see out there?" She squeezed my shoulder once, twice.

"I guess." *Did I?*

"Well, I hope so, because it's gonna be a cold winter as is. I couldn't bear to bury you, too." She sighed heavily. "Child, I need you to look at me."

I turned to her. I've always loved her face. We used to rub our cheeks together—just like soft, cool silk.

"Now, hear me good. Out there"—she jerked her thumb back in the direction we'd just come from—"they doing whatever it is they do, suffering whatever it is they need to suffer. Let them alone."

"But, Gran," I wailed like a baby, "I only saw Hannah."

She let out a long whistling sound of relief. "That's about all the ghost you can handle right now." She looked at me hard. "Did she tell you anything?"

"What?! Aren't you supposed to be telling me I didn't see anything? That it was just my imagination?"

Gran only raised an eyebrow and sucked her teeth in response.

"Why would I see Hannah when I can't even

picture Marianne's face in my head?" I asked, exasperated. "There's something wrong with that!"

"No, honey," Gran said, looking at me like I was the most pitiful thing on earth. "There ain't nothing wrong with that. You just trying too hard now. Trying to bring her back. You only see what you're ready to see." She reached over the back seat and took my face in her hands. "Black folks got enough ghosts in this country to be haunted till the end of time. Why you want to haunt yourself with the one ghost that's trying to leave you in peace?"

"All I ever wanted . . ." I began to tell her everything—how M and I used to kiss long after we knew better under the blackberry bush in the woods, how it was M who kissed me first, kissed me for real, but how I never wanted it to stop. How her Mamm had caught me sneaking into M's room more than once, trying to get her to talk to me even though M had already told me she didn't love me like that, didn't want me to come back—but I caught myself. I had never told any of this to anybody before. But it wasn't like M would have the chance to push me away again.

"All there ever was for me . . . was her."

I couldn't even look up into Gran's face.

"Girl," she said sympathetically, maybe even

slightly exasperatedly, "I know that. Been knowing that. The first time you all set eyes on one another you were stuck together like ants in molasses. There was always something special between you two. And you didn't think I knew what you all were doing under that blackberry bush?"

Gran was dropping serious bombshells. "Why didn't you say something?"

She looked at me seriously. "Opal, if I told you everything I knew you wouldn't be able to shut your mouth for a week. 'Sides, not like you was ever really good at keeping it a secret." She handed me some tissues like that'd make everything better. "Now let's go in and pick up some things."

"Gran, I can't. It's too . . . ugly. I can't stand it."

The place made me ill. She'd driven a good hour and twenty minutes to get to this consumer amusement park. More like a house of horrors to me. It had its own particular aroma that lingered on the things you bought. Not to mention how the fluorescent lights sucked all the life out of my eyes. Not to mention the memories.

Gran looked hard at me. "I'm not trying to chase you anymore, Little Girl. You stay in this car, hear?"

"Course." I shrugged. Not like I asked anybody

to come looking for me anyway. Not like I was even running away *from* something. Just maybe running to.

Gran locked up the car and went around checking all the doors, pulling on the handles like it was Fort Knox and she could actually keep me locked in. I lay back in the seat and closed my eyes. What was going to keep all those memories locked out?

❧ ❧ ❧

I woke from faceless dreams having to pee real bad. Gran had been in there a half-hour already, which meant it could be a half-hour more. Which meant I was going to have to go inside. Damn my body. It never worked the way I wanted it to.

Just in and out. That was all it would take. Run, piss, run. That was it. Maybe I wouldn't even have to open my eyes. I knew there was a bathroom right by the door, next to the big yellow and red scary-faced clown man who welcomed all the little sheep to eat his fast and nasty suicide chow.

The automatic doors opened with a huge sucking sound. I was smacked with that specially fabricated odor that always triggered some kind of purge—all the money from your wallet at the very least. I pulled my hat down so my eyelashes brushed against the bill. But the glare of the fluorescent lights reflecting off the polished floor still made me squint and scowl. People were shuffling all around me, with somebody shouting into the intercom, "Assistance in sporting goods! Can someone please assist a customer with the semiautomatic rifles?"

Just move, girl. Run, piss, run. That was it.

RESTROOM CLOSED
FOR MAINTENANCE.
PLEASE EXCUSE THIS
INCONVIENCE AND USE
THE FACILITIES AT THE
REAR OF THE STORE.

If I didn't have to pee so badly, I'd spit on the stupid smiley face on the misspelled sign. The rear of the store was at the other end of the universe, but I was going to get there as fast as I could. Only thing about this place: You couldn't run too fast or security might tackle you. Still, the brilliant products, the blank-eyed people, all blurred past me. I might've even broken a record for speed walking.

I finished in record time, too. Had to shove three old biddies out my way, but you know what they say: Times are tough, kids are mean. Figured I'd try to find Gran so she didn't send out a SWAT team for me. I kept to the very back aisle, looking down each perpendicular row of neatly stacked crap. Then it started to get to me—the lights, the smell, the shine, the people. All the people. Pushing, shouting, whining, looking. Couldn't help but feel like I was in slow motion. Muzak zigzagged down from the ceiling, sounding as if it had been handpicked by a team of brainwashing experts.

100   I started to feel like a zombie. The weight of this death was pulling down on me. Everything was a memory. Even the freaking yarn aisle. The first time we had come here. We had still been wild when this place first opened. Think I had some rocks I'd picked up and decided were magic loaded in my back pocket. Gran had to pull some leaves and feathers out of M's hair just before we walked in. We were in terror and awe until we found the best way to deal with a place that seemed like a morgue after a day in the forest.

SEVEN

W<small>E WERE</small> soaring down the yarn aisle on our knees (Marianne's idea), just like we did at Shallow Lake every winter after the hard freeze. Running and then dropping to our knees. Again and again, the purples, greens, and pinks sliding past us until we ran out of momentum. Our yellow and brown hands clasped, thrown up high. Gran had long given up trying to get us to another aisle, so she'd moved on, checking on us every now and then. Besides, it was keeping us from asking her when we were leaving.

At some point, we noticed two girls standing there giggling, watching us. Pretty red ribbons dangled from their pigtails, brushing against their strawberry-shortcake complexions as they laughed. They were dressed exactly alike, but one seemed taller and older than us.

"Hey," M said, brushing off her knees as she got up. Always the friendly one. I wasn't done sliding. I took off and did it again, even though my knees and shins felt like they might be bleeding under my overalls. Before we had come, Gran had made me put on a shirt, and I was still feeling sour over that. The sliding was helping to turn my mood.

When I finally got up and turned around, the two girls were on either side of M, like they were examining her. I could feel her getting uncomfortable—she was looking back and forth between them—so I went over.

"Our mama said not to play with blacks," the tall one was saying. "You black, too?" She yanked a piece of Marianne's hair. Gran had braided it in cornrows, just like mine.

"What *are* you, anyway?" She was in Marianne's face now. I got in between them. Even though this girl was bigger, nobody was picking on M if I could help it.

Still, the question hung in the air like the foul synthetic stench of the place. Threw everything off kilter. What was she? That was a question I'd never thought to ask—it was the first time I'd even considered it. She was M, Mlapo, Marianne. What else did she need to be?

The girl asked again, as if I wasn't standing there in front of her face, my hands clenched in fists, like she couldn't even see me. "What *are* you?"

I looked back at Marianne. I could see her confusion; she'd apparently never thought about it, either. When she looked into my eyes, she found what sounded to me like a good answer.

"I'm like her," she said, her best and only offering.

"No. No, you ain't," the girl insisted, her red ribbons flailing, wormlike. Her nostrils flared as she talked. I could see the tiny delicate hairs inside her pink nose. Her breath smelled like peppermint. The younger one was bobbing her head in agreement, her mouth slightly open so I could see the red and white striped candy lolling around in there.

"If you was black, you'd be dark like *her*." This was the only time she addressed me. "But you ain't white, neither. So what *are* you?"

M's mouth hung open like a nut-less nutcracker. I tried to think of words to fill that space, to make this girl, her ribbons, and her senseless questions all disappear. This was territory we'd never thought to explore. Sure, there weren't many folks in town who looked like either of us, but we were never around them much. Gran kept us mostly to ourselves—we were still being homeschooled then. What was this blackness and whiteness that meant so much to this girl? What did it matter? Why was it so important?

"You can't get away with tryin' to be white if you ain't," the girl said, as if it were a law we were caught breaking. She stood on her tiptoes, towering over us even more. "And if I was you, I wouldn't go around telling people you was black, either." She squinted her eyes until all I could see were her eyelashes, knitted curtains hiding her pupils. "So why don't you know what you are?"

M's face changed three or four times before she sputtered, "I . . . I know who I am!" I grabbed her hand and we tore out of there, trying to leave that pain behind us.

We ended up not being able to find Gran in the maze of the store. We hid behind some tall, fake foliage instead. It was the closest thing to familiar in the whole place. I held M as she cried and I growled at anyone who came near. Gran finally found us when someone screeched over the intercom, "If anyone is missing two children, could you please pick them up in the houseplant department? They're scaring our other customers."

Embarrassed by the crowd we'd managed to

amass, Gran yanked us out of there without asking what happened. All the way home she just went on and on about how she couldn't take us anywhere without our acting like wild banshees and causing a ruckus. I couldn't help but steal glances at Marianne, who was refusing to respond, even to me. I watched her, for the first time realizing that there were things about her that I'd never know. Wondering what other questions about her I couldn't answer myself.

❧ ❧ ❧

I slid down the aisle. Full run, then a drop to the knees. Purples, greens, yellows, pinks, flew past until I ran out of momentum. But my dumb teary eyes blurred the scene. Before the last time I saw her, it struck me— when was the last time I had seen M cry? No matter how hard they'd tried to squeeze her into their tiny labeled boxes. But had she really put up a fight? I shook my head to get that thought out, got up, and did the routine again. Any fast flight burned the pain away. She had taught me that.

"Sir! Sir, you can't do that in here!" a voice behind me barked.

That couldn't have been meant for me. Sure, I'm the last one you'd ever call girlie, but whoever it was couldn't have been talking to me.

"Sir? Did you hear what I said?"

I stood, brushing off my knees, my thighs, my hips, my breasts. I looked down at myself: steel-toe boots dribbled with paint, baggy brown overalls (not much had changed since back when I was six), plaid flannel shirt underneath, a big, ratty navy pea coat from the surplus store thrown around my shoulders as a cape for flying, green corduroy truckers' hat, not much hair to be seen.

I froze.

Now that he was asking, I couldn't find an answer on my tongue. Like something on a chalkboard but now erased.

What are *you, anyway?* Knocking around like a pinball in my head.

I'm like her. Two pinballs now.

I turned.

Just me and this dude standing in the aisle.

He saw me, all of me, and his face changed like he had just grabbed hold of a rope made of sand. His expression adjusted with recognition that I wasn't a sir. I backed away, three paces, four.

"I know who I am!" I shouted, knocking skeins of yarn onto the floor.

Eight

"Gran!"

I ran up just as she was peering into the car.

"Little Girl!" she said, turning quickly with relief in her voice. She'd been leaning on the shopping cart and it began rolling away. I steadied Gran by the elbow with one hand and caught the runaway cart with the other. Guess I had startled her.

107

"See, child?" She held my chin between her thumb and forefinger. "See? What am I going to do without you? I look in this car and where are you? Not here. My heart stopped. Then! Then you come flyin' in from nowhere. Saved my life."

"Oh, stop," I said, shaking my face out of her hand. "You old drama queen! Almost had me!"

She continued to stare me down, but I grabbed up some of the bags and began noisily loading up the car. I just didn't want to hear it. Didn't want to hear any of it.

Gran sat in the car as I put the cart away. I had to sit in the front with her because of all she'd bought. We rode almost the whole way back in silence, with the gray sky melting away into the dark. Johnny Mathis was still singing away on the tape deck.

"Chances are—you believe the stars that fill the skies are in my eyes . . ."

Oh, Johnny. I wouldn't bet on it if I were you.

As we got closer to the house, the trees began turning into the familiar black giants I knew so well, leaning against the late November twilight. No more twilights for Marianne. I hugged myself, trying to keep everything inside.

Gran flipped the headlights on, drawing my attention to her.

"Girl, I know right now you just want to think about yourself and her. I understand that. When your grandaddy died I felt the same way. Everydamnbody said I'd get over it in time, but that just made me feel worse, like a traitor to his memory." She kept her eyes on the road; her fingers gripped and released the baby blue steering wheel.

"But you got to know that my heart's broke,

too," she continued. "Not just for her. Or even just for myself. I've got to keep reminding myself she's gone for good. But my heart's broke for you, too. I know what she was to you. You remember all she was to *us?* You remember all *you* is to us?" Her usually deep, steady voice broke a bit. Broke a bit of me, too.

"This ain't just you going through this alone. Just so you know."

I wanted to tell her that nobody knew anything. That I could say things to make her cry. I had a whole forest full of secrets to lose her in. I could tell them all things they'd cry to forget. What did anyone know about what we were? Nobody knew anything but me.

"We need you to keep breathing, girl. That's how we'll keep her with us—through you."

Want me to keep living like this? Her memory was pounding on my brain. And no matter how hard I tried, how much I wanted, I couldn't recall what her face looked like, even the moment before she left me. Only her hands. Fitted together to make a blackbird against the sun.

Gran kept talking about keeping people alive with stories and memories. I was only half listening, but next thing I knew, she was telling that old slave story again. I watched the darkness eat up the world outside the window as she talked.

※ ※ ※

They reached Mine's people having walked entirely through the woods and mostly in darkness with Mine's keen direction, keeping far away from towns and farms. They had crossed the wide bay in a canoe Mine had hidden in the woods on his journey to meet and trade goods with the older Indian, whose people were called Patuxent. Mine had found her clinging to that old tree, which was the exact spot at which he and his friend always met at that time of the season.

They were welcomed with smiles and hugs. There weren't many of the Nanticokes left, but they lived as well as they could. Mine introduced Hannah to his mother; she was an old woman, blind now, but she held Hannah tight when they greeted.

Although Hannah didn't want to put these giving people in danger with her own troubles, she couldn't bear to think of leaving Mine. They lived together now as husband and wife. Hannah had

had no idea that someone could catch hold of her like that—she'd had no idea about love and what that kind of safety was like. How new, how nice it sounded to her ears and tongue: the word we. He treated her as if she was a priceless part of him, and she treated him the same.

They spent a few weeks mostly alone but together; he showed her everything about his life, his world. They went digging for clams, fishing, and hunting for themselves, his mother, and anyone else who was hungry. They helped to farm the crops that grew in the woods. It was so good to eat food that wasn't just scraps or leftovers from someone else. It was something to be free. Mine laughed when Hannah said this, said that this was not even as free as his people had once been.

At that time there was a man visiting the village, a cousin from the North. He was urging the people to come to Pennsylvania and live with the rest of the clan. Mine told Hannah that before he had met her, he hadn't liked the idea of leaving the land—they'd been pushed away from their ancestors' lands in Maryland already. He told her that not very long ago, his people had had *many villages across the entire area the whites now called Maryland and Delaware. They had hunted, farmed, and camped inland in the cold months and by the shore in the warm. They came and went as they pleased. Now, if they left their homes for hunting season, the whites would often take the land as their own. The cousin said that the Pennsylvania Quakers made life easier on the Indian and on the black, that it was a state where they could all live undisturbed. Mine said he didn't know how much he trusted any of these "states" and "laws" to be much different from any others. Hannah agreed but reminded him that she was still a fugitive. She knew she needed to get as far away from Maryland as she could. Mine told Hannah that he would not let her go without him. So they made the decision to move farther north together. His mother refused to go, said she was tired of running, of fighting. Mine mourned many nights over this, but also knew in his heart she wouldn't survive another long, hard trip. He knew he would never see her again. Hannah never knew her real mother but reckoned losing one after so long was worse, and she grieved with him.*

Weeks after they left Mine's people, they were back in the thick woods, headed northwest on a very old trail Mine called Shamokin, toward a camp his people used—Punxsutawney (it meant "Land of the Sand Flies"). As with most of their ancestors' lands, whites occupied most of the area, but Mine said he thought they could keep out of sight if they stayed in the forest. Hannah didn't mind at all—she was learning to feel safe surrounded by trees.

They'd decided not to travel with the rest of the group, who would be moving slowly, heavy with children and belongings. Also, Hannah feared being recognized as a fugitive and causing trouble for everyone. They had only each other, but neither Hannah nor Mine was complaining. Although they walked most nights, they sometimes felt comfortable enough in the woods to set up shelter and stay in one spot for a day or two. They never saw any sign of people as they approached the summit of the mountain. As the weather got colder, they had to stop more and more, and both began to worry about the winter. When she woke one morning and the ground was covered with frost, Hannah was grateful that Mine's mother had given her the yellowed buckskin shawl she'd always worn while traveling between their winter and summer camps.

During that cold spell, they finally found shelter—their own tiny wigwam, as Mine called it, built against a nook in the side of the mountain. Mine said they'd be safe in it until the weather cleared and they could travel again, but they both felt downhearted to even think about trudging onward. Although they loved each other's company, traveling as they did, with few supplies, was difficult. They tried hard not to think about someone coming back to claim the cabin, and each said a silent prayer that, if the owner did come back, it wouldn't be too soon.

The wigwam had a hearth with an iron pot in the corner—not much, but just what they needed. Mine thought it might even be an old shelter left by his people. As they made themselves comfortable, building a little fire and eating what was left of their dried meat supply, they couldn't help but want to stay, to make it a home. While they'd walked, they'd both daydreamed and talked about when they'd have their own place, when they could stop running and settle. But

after many talks and several days' rest, they knew
they would have to keep going. Mine reasoned
that the farther north they got before making a
more permanent winter camp, the better.

❧ ❧ ❧

The next thing I knew, Gran was pulling into our long drive, the new shocks riding smoothly over the chunks of buckling asphalt. I could see the house lights through the circle of trees surrounding the house. Gran pulled around the bend, up to the front. I remembered all the packages in the back, realized why there was so much stuff . . .

"You better know I need you, Little Girl," Gran said.

If I could have seen behind the far side of the house from here, I figured there'd be a car. Judging from all of the groceries Gran had picked up, probably even the rig. With the headlights off, the darkness shuffled in around us. One patch of sky was torn open, bleeding the last bit of sunset.

Gran opened the car door and light flooded the interior—the assault of baby blue. I squinted and turned my head. She slammed the door quickly and the darkness was cooling again. I watched her go into the house, heard her raise her voice to greet someone.

For this quick second I considered running. Go to the forest and let it take me. Let the leaves blanket me. Let the trees lift me up to the stars. I wanted to go to our little secret hiding place in the blackberry bush. I wanted to go back to where everything was sweet.

I didn't want anybody to need me. I didn't even want to need myself.

I clicked the switch on the ceiling so I could open the door without the light. I stepped out, the wind chimes in the trees calling out in clattering unison. I crossed the front of the house crouching, almost making it to the utter darkness of the woods; the treetops beckoned. But then I saw something moving, just on the very edge of the woods. Like a tree with arms and legs. I stepped back. The creaking of the back screen door turned my attention to the house and a figure standing half in, half out of the light.

"Opal?" Mama's voice. Always sounded like she was singing my name. I looked back to where I'd seen the walking tree. Pops stood there now, his dark, strong features softly lit by the house lights. And then more lights through the trees, coming around the bend—a car. The left light blinking as the car hit a bump. Oh, Lordy, the El Camino.

Pops caught me in less than three steps. My knees had buckled at the sight of the figure stepping out of the car. In my mind I had been running to her, thinking it was Marianne. My body had had other plans— like running in the opposite direction when I had seen it was Mary. Must've looked a funny sight, because when Pops had me in his arms all I could hear was his deep rumble of a laugh as he held me close to his chest.

"That's no way to treat a guest, now, is it, O?"

My ear buzzed as he spoke quietly, his head bent. Suddenly I was feeling like a baby again. Safe.

117

Pops was my giant, my tree. He knew me in ways that neither of us had to say. I rested my head on his chest and instantly felt our heartbeats in sync.

"Bring her in, then," I heard Mama say with a sigh in her voice.

Squeezing my arms, he brought me to my feet. Held me so close to him that I barely had to walk.

"Time to face the music, kid," he said, bending to speak in my ear. "I'm right here with you."

✌ ✌ ✌

Ah, the tears. There had never been much crying in

this house, but suddenly we were all pros. I didn't have to worry about looking anyone in the eye—the tears were blinding enough. Everything was a blur of movement and color.

Mama pulled me away from Pops as soon as we got into the house. Folded me into her like a precious letter. She smelled like a combination of her lemon verbena perfume and the olive oil that she rubbed into her skin to make it glisten—smelled like dessert and dinner all at the same time. Always said that was how she'd caught Pops.

She kissed me all over my face, then cried and yelled at me for running to the woods and scaring Gran. I couldn't do anything but blubber like a baby. This was precisely what I hated about family: They could see your weaknesses. And they were always telling you about them.

I could hear Pops's deep voice farther down the hall, telling her to give me a break. Mama put me in the kitchen, where Drippy's denture-glue breath caught me. His hands were squarely on my shoulders. As he pressed me quickly to himself in an awkward hug, an ocean of country-scent dryer sheets wrapped around me. Was it just a few days ago that she had come into the Drip 'n' Drop?

"You're both like my own," he mumbled, patting me on the back. "You know that."

Yeah, I knew that. So what? So what to all of this? Why couldn't they all just forget me and let me alone? Instead, they all just wanted to make me cry, telling me things. Drips led me to a chair, but it was Gran's hands that made me sit—carrying a bowl of her homemade chicken soup.

"And my sources tell me that you been eatin' at that so-called establishment over town," Gran huffed as she put the bowl in front of me. "What'd I tell you? That kind of slop won't do you no good. Witch 'prolly poisoned you, all I know."

That could have been true, but I didn't really care. I wouldn't have eaten the soup, but Gran stood there and made sure I did. Pops came into the kitchen when I was about halfway through. He palmed my head in my hat. The tips of his fingers almost reached inside my ears.

"You ready?" he asked. I tried to shake my head no but his grip wouldn't let me. Gran told him I had to finish my soup.

"She got other folks to see, Ma," he said in a voice reserved only for her. She, on the other hand, did not reserve any voice for him.

"Don't you think I know? Tryin' to give this girl some sustenance, son."

"Yes, ma'am."

But I didn't have any choice. He led me into the family room, as Gran called it. Pops skillfully peeled me off him and sat me down on the couch. I didn't want to let my daddy go. I knew who I was being set down next to. I didn't even have to wipe my eyes. The heavy odor of Jean Naté body splash sprinkled with baby powder told me exactly who it was.

NINE

"My girl's gone" was all she said.

I mustered only a nod. Tears and snot were soaking up my clothes.

"Some a them sayin' she did it to herself."

I was glad at that moment that I was just doing a good impression of a faucet, instead of any loud sobbing or crying. Tonight Mary was quiet as a church mouse. She sat there smoking with the window open (Gran's doing, I was sure), the cold night sinking its teeth into us. I could feel Mary shivering, quaking the space between our bodies, and it was catching. I pulled my knees up to my chest and prepared for a crash landing.

"You know somethin' I need to know?" She blew smoke in my direction and it clamped around my throat.

I prolonged my coughing fit in order to think about what she'd said. What did Mary *really* need to know? The last time we'd seen each other, she was kicking me out of a window, calling me names in Dutch that I'm sure all meant the same thing. Telling me I'd corrupted *her* daughter. The thought made me cough louder and longer to keep me from laughing. She'd be sitting here longer than she thought. A lot longer, if I told her just half of what I knew. And what I knew about M's state of mind was a lot less clear to me than I'd ever let anyone think.

I had to stop coughing and say something before Gran came in to make me reach my arms up into the air while she pounded on my back.

"Nope," I lied, clearing my throat. "Nothin' you need to know." *Or want to know, for that matter.*

She busied herself smoothing the pleats on her black miniskirt. I'd seen Marianne wearing it once or twice last year when she'd dressed up as a naughty Catholic schoolgirl. Now I could see Mary's varicose veins underneath her stockings—she'd always cursed M because she got them from being pregnant.

On many occasions Mary would tell Marianne: "I'd still have the prettiest gams in all a PA if you weren't around, kid."

Varicose veins or not, Mary still had the legs of a narcoleptic magician's assistant, as Gran would say. Whatever that meant.

Oh, our Mary was a stunner. Where Marianne's hair was wild and dusty yellow like a lion's mane, Mary's was a smooth panther black. She usually wore it pulled back tight so her sharp features would show more. But today, I saw as I wiped my eyes that she'd done it for the funeral. If I ever had to guess why Mary and Jinx had left the Amish, I'd say it was for Mary's vanity and pride. Her hair was teased and coifed like she'd stepped out of a Miss America pageant, representin' for Miss PA. The naturally pale rosy hue of her skin was softened by the table lamp's circle of smoky light. Still, she had the look of a farm girl—like she could up and midwife a cow at the drop of a hat and not even change facial expressions. This was the first time I'd ever seen her so still and quiet. It was a little scary.

She nodded like she agreed with me. "Then why's Sheriff telling me she had drugs on her? Why'm I finding this out from him?" Taking a long drag of her cigarette, she skillfully flipped the butt out the window. "If there's nothing I need to know from *you?*"

Oh yeah. The drugs. I gripped the cushion. This

was exactly why I didn't want to go through this. Explanations sucked, especially when you were fresh out of them. And the tears had finally decided to take a hike, so I couldn't play that card anymore. But at least I could answer this one question honestly.

"Just found out myself," I said, mostly to the couch. "Hadn't seen her . . . for a while now." I could feel her studying my face as I studied the nappy carpet. Her steady gaze drew my eyes up to hers.

"I know 'xactly what you mean," Mary said after a moment, lighting another cigarette. I could see then that she had something clenched in her hand—it almost looked as if it were tattooed there: a picture of her and Marianne. She turned her hand up and looked at it and exhaled with a sigh that ended as a deep moan. It was the same sound my heart had made every time I'd ever looked at Marianne's face.

The sound of longing. Of unquenchable need.

❧ ❧ ❧

Gran placed herself between us, mostly to comfort Mary but also to grab her cigarette before it burned the carpet. Mama came in to get in on the act, too. I jumped up as soon as I saw Pops motion in my direction. I didn't know how to react—my mouth had fallen open. How Marianne would have laughed. And cried. She'd wanted her whole life to see her mother act out any emotion toward her. Nobody ever really questioned that Mary loved her, but to see that love? To feel that love? That was just the way Mary was, a good face but not much feeling underneath. It wasn't a crime or anything. Marianne got plenty of kisses and hugs over here, but in her own house . . .

As a baby she'd been held and cradled, like most babies, probably a little more because she'd never fall asleep without being held by her granddad, Jinx, until she was a year old. He'd sing her a little song in his language and she'd pass right out. I always remembered the tune, it was so pretty—sometimes, as we got older, she'd hum it to herself as she drifted off to sleep. But once she was able to walk and handle most things on her own, Marianne had little physical contact with her Mamm or Jinx.

Before the stroke, Jinx showered M with love in other ways. He made all of her bedroom furniture by hand and to her exact specifications. Taught her how to drive around in the farm equipment for fun when she was seven, tied bricks to her feet so she could reach the pedals. He somehow saved up enough money to buy her an off-road motorbike when she turned ten.

Man, we had some kind of fun on that thing!

After Mary had to change professions, things really began to get bad for M at home. One of Mary's poker-party regulars, a rowdy trucker we knew only as Uncle, started calling M Penny when he was around. Eventually, the other men did, too, and then other folks in town caught on and for a while it stuck. We never thought about why they never said it in front of any of my family. For a year M bragged it was because of her pretty complexion.

But it wasn't. One night, Uncle was over with a few others, playing poker while M and I were hanging out in her room. I don't know how I was over there when all this was going on—usually Gran didn't leave me with Mary for too long, especially not overnight. I think it must have been the time Drippy took Gran to Pittsburgh to help some sick friend of hers, but I'm pretty sure she didn't know there'd be a kitchen full of gambling men involved.

Up in M's room, we could smell the cigars and cigarettes and hear the men's booming laughter and carrying-on wafting through the floorboards. Every once in a while, Mary's voice rose above their low tones like the very last note on the toy xylophone we had banged on as babies. I was sitting on the bed, M was dancing around and doing hairbrush karaoke to one of her Mamm's Janis Joplin tapes—she was always putting on some kind of show for me, way before I even knew why I liked to watch her so much. I remember how she was excited to have me over at her house for the whole night.

"I betcha we could get a beer from downstairs," she said in the middle of her not-yet-perfected round-off cartwheel. Back then, she was just beginning to put together the idea that getting on the cheerleading squad would be her one-way express ticket to Popularville, where life was easy and everybody was nice. We were just about to go into middle school and were getting a little tired of the outcast routine, but for me anything was bearable as long as I had M. We were both so young and dumb it didn't occur to us that the other girls on the squad might not welcome me with open arms. I was thinking I'd be right there with her (now I thought, *where?* As captain of the football team? More like the water boy. Damn, I was stupid). By then she'd stopped asking Gran to put her hair in cornrows like mine and was always wearing pigtails instead.

I shrugged, not really that curious. Pops always gave me a sip of his Miller Lite when he was home. I preferred the taste of blackberries.

"C'mon," she whined, as if she'd have to fight me to get anything she asked for. "Sometimes they let me have one or two if I sit on Uncle's lap and ask real nice. Then he gets me one from the fridge when Mamm's not looking."

Downstairs was a hazy gray that made me instantly want to be outside. The stale air made bluish halos around the men's heads. I recognized a few of them—Charlie and some others from town. M's Mamm was in the living room—-there was music and her giggle that ended with a hiccup—but we couldn't see her.

"Well, well. Lookie what we have here," Uncle drawled as we stepped into the kitchen, as if he were from Memphis instead of Allentown. The other men paused but quickly returned to their game.

"Well now, how's my lil' Penny?"

He caught Marianne's wrist in his hand, circled it with just his pinky and thumb. I could see the calluses on the inside of his palm. I wondered what they were from. He pulled her up to straddle his knee and began bouncing her like a newborn. M giggled like her mother.

"Her, too." She pointed at me. I stood there stupidly, trying out my best imitation of the wall-paper.

Uncle was bouncing her so much, Marianne sounded as if she had a little motor inside of her, jiggling her voice.

"Well, two's better than one, I always say." Uncle chortled. He reached over and pulled me onto his other leg. At first it was kind of funny. I giggled, too. Soon it got harder to keep from sliding off. Uncle was holding on to our wrists, then our arms. Then his hands were on our thighs, squeezing. Through it all, Uncle kept grinning, his eyes closed and his head leaning back like he was on a beach somewhere nice. One of the men asked if he was in or out of the game, and Uncle told him he was busy without opening his eyes or stopping the steady motion of his legs. The men kept on playing.

"M?" I whispered, trying to get her attention. But she was just staring over Uncle's shoulder into the living room where her Mamm's giggles had turned suddenly quiet.

"M!" I was beginning to feel seasick. I was way over this ride. The smoke in the room was stealing my breath, making my mouth dry. My teeth felt like they were rattling around in my brain.

Marianne finally looked at me when Uncle's squeezing hands felt like he was trying to take pieces of us away with him. I was trying to squirm out of his grasp, but he just kept on like it was a part of the game and held us closer to his basketball belly.

"Hey, Uncle," M finally piped up, "can we please have a beer? Mamm's not looking now."

"Well, Penny darlin', you sure can," he said, his face barely changing expression. "In just two shakes of a lamb's tail . . ." His voice trailed off as he changed the tempo to less bounce, more jiggle.

"Uncle!" Mary spoke up, suddenly standing at the threshold, untwisting her skirt. Past her in the living room I could see one of the sheriff's deputies buttoning his shirt.

130   The bouncing stopped and his hands unlocked. I couldn't get down fast enough and ended up falling to the linoleum floor with a thud. A couple of the men looked down at me without offering a hand. Marianne still sat on his lap like a posable baby doll.

"Uncle! What did I tell you last time 'bout jostling my child?" Mary spoke in a voice that was more like begging than asking a question. "They *supposed* to be upstairs, asleep. You want her to puke on you again? I don't want to have to explain nothing to this one's granny. And neither do you." She barely glanced at me.

"Well, a course not. We was all just having us some fun." Uncle hung his head like a sad old dog caught stealing scraps from the table. But I could see his smirk from where I'd landed on the floor. "Ain't that right, pretty Penny?"

M nodded mechanically, her eyes on her mother and the deputy still fumbling with his shirt. Mary went back into the living room to assist the deputy.

"And you know I don't like you callin' her that . . ." Mary's voice ended up muffled.

Uncle carefully placed Marianne on her feet. I got myself up. He went to the fridge and held two beers out to her, got a third for himself, then patted her head and sat back down to the game.

We walked slowly down the hall toward the stairs up to her room. I slid along the wall, trying to wipe off some of what I was feeling. M was jabbering about what she wanted for her twelfth birthday, only a few weeks away, as she peeled back the shiny metal ring on the can, slipping it onto her finger. We stopped so she could take a sip of the froth that bubbled out. The men's laughter filled the house. I could feel it vibrating in the walls. I put the can M had handed me to my forehead, trying to cool my thoughts.

"What d'you call her Penny for?" We stopped, hearing one of the men, a stranger to me, ask the question.

Uncle boomed out a hearty laugh. He lowered his voice, so M stopped drinking her beer to listen.

"Well, I'll put it to ya this way: You know what her mama is, a course?"

"Yeah."

"Well, by the looks of her, you know who her daddy is, right?"

"I heard that nobody knows who, but we certainly all knows *what*."

They both laughed at that.

"Well, when you add it all up, she may be pretty, but she can't be worth more than a penny!"

All the men around the table roared with laughter this time.

For the first time ever in our lives, it was hard for me to look at M. When I did, she was already done with her beer and was reaching for mine.

"I know who I am," she said quietly, her voice wavering. Her smile was crooked, her left eyetooth only half grown in. Yanking back the tab, she leaned her head back and took several gulps. She looked me dead in the eye.

"I know," she said again, her chin quivering, but her voice steady and clear.

Pops led me away from what shall now be forever known as The Scene: Mama, Gran, and Mary all huddled up together, crying, holding, and pulling on each other. It was all genuine, but it was, like, *ancient*— I mean, somebody should've been there to carve their three images out of stone or paint their contrasts in a grand and vivid scene. But it was just our family room, and they were only mothers, each related differently to the same dead child.

Pops led me through the back door. The air outside sucked away at my breath. He sat me out on what we called our "star chairs," where he and I would sit for hours in silence, staring up at the twinkling velvet soup. It was a perfect spot to see Orion, the warrior, our favorite constellation. But there were no stars out tonight. Pops had the huge, heavy wool carpet we always used as a blanket, and he threw it over me.

I gave him a sidelong glance; didn't he need some warmth?

He raised one shoulder, tilted his head; he'd be all right.

And we sat. Watched the nothing, the dark. So much quiet outside, it made some space for quiet inside. Leave it to my Pops to know exactly what I needed.

A long while passed. Just as my teeth started chattering, the back door opened, piercing the peace with a shard of reality. Drippy stuck his head out, a silent message from Gran not to let me stay out and catch cold.

Pops cocked his head in the direction of the house. *Time to go back, girl.*

I bit my lip. *Do I have to?*

He nodded only once, like his head weighed a thousand pounds.

❦ ❦ ❦

I went to my room, or what used to be my room. Chanteuse had turned my desk into her own personal mini salon. Scarves of various colors, patterns, and glitz were draped everywhere. Her 10X-magnification self-lit tri-folding mirror was propped on one of my science textbooks. Chanteuse's makeup toolbox (I wouldn't have been surprised to find a wrench in there, too) was open on top of some antique maps of Pennsylvania Pops had sent me not too long ago. I went about trying to salvage my space but had to quit when one of the fake eyelashes attacked me.

I turned toward my bed, shoving a bunch of dresses out of the way so I could stretch out. My muscles were tight from the cold and the day. What a day. I lay down, about to break into tears again, when I noticed something on the night table next to me—a piece of mail. It was from Stanford. How ironic that it had come today. I thought about ripping the white envelope open or maybe tearing it to shreds. Not so sure I really wanted to read what was in it. Its contents, whatever they were, seemed inconsequential now, though a little voice inside my head wanted to know if . . . But even *if* it was an acceptance letter, why go? I should just stay here, keep working for Drippy and taking care of Gran, and maybe go to Penn State later or something. I didn't want to think about later just yet.

The envelope beside me looked so crisp, so official. I hid it under the mattress.

I tiptoed out the back door again, hearing Mama, Gran, and Mary talking in the kitchen. I could see Pops's shape, still sitting in the star chair. He had finally covered himself with the huge rug, but his legs stuck out considerably. Figuring he was napping, I slipped next to him quietly. I was startled when he pulled the rug over me. We sat like that for a long time.

"You know about the Pleiades?" he said, his breath giving a white outline to the shapes of the trees.

"Of course," I said, following his gaze upward to

a small patch of sky that had suddenly opened itself up to us. A tiny fierce cluster of sister stars all winked like the light in a glamour puss's eye.

"Or Aldebaran? You know that one? Right there behind the ladies, the Pleiades. Aldebaran means 'the follower' in Arabic. Bet you don't know about him."

He was right. Not far to the left of the soft, glittery lights was a glowing red fist of a star, looking like it was after something. There were other star clusters between Aldebaran and Pleiades, blocking its arrowlike precision, perfectly aligned for a cosmic crash course. Pops had gotten me into star watching when I was a kid, so by now I knew most of the stories of the stars from mythology. But this was one he hadn't named before.

"Story is, our friend Aldebaran's only objective is to love the beautiful Pleiades," Pops continued. The only time he ever talked so much at a stretch was when he talked about the stars.

"But poor Aldebaran is too scared—he never gets close enough, always follows along blindly. Not blind from the beauty of the Pleiades, but blind to his own. He's the very eye of the constellation Taurus, the bull, but Aldebaran the follower can look only to the allure of the Pleiades. Never sees himself. Never sees his worth, never takes the chance."

As Pops sat up, the patch of clear night shut itself up again. He turned his head toward me. I could feel him looking at me hard in the darkness, but I couldn't clearly see his face. He stood, reaching his long arms above him, swirling his hands in the dark. He reached down for my hand, pulled me up, and hugged me.

"Look to the stars," he said, and held me for a moment. "They'll keep you steady." He let go and pushed me back in the direction of the house. "Tell your mamas I'll be in shortly."

Ten

I walked into the house, thinking of what Pops had said. As I went toward the kitchen, I heard Mama yell out.

"Old woman, you a cheat!"

And Mary's voice: "This why I stop coming here!"

I went in cautiously, expecting to see somebody in a chokehold. But the three of them were sitting around the table, playing Skip-Bo. When we were kids, even though Gran held many a grudge, she'd play that card game with just about anyone. M and I would leave for school in the morning and come back in the afternoon to still find the three of them knee-deep in the game. But I hadn't seen it out for a minute.

Skip-Bo was one of those games that had to be

played to learn. And at this point, the three of them had strategies against each other that still baffled me. I could tell that Gran was winning, despite Mama and Mary's combined efforts to defeat her. But in all likelihood, Gran had probably been cheating all along.

I stood close to Mama and she wrapped her arm around my hips, leaned her head against my belly. Mary was reshuffling the discard deck and shaking her head, making a *tsk, tsk* sound with her tongue.

"Now that Little Girl's here," Gran said seriously, "we should start again and play teams this time. If you all so concerned I'm not playing fair."

"I don't think so." Mama snorted. "Put the two of you together and it'll be rigged for sure!" She and Mary fell out laughing.

"Remember how she used to give the girls candy for cheating their own mothers?" Mary asked, clutching her sides. "Poor things almost went into sugar shock before we figured it out!" Then she stopped laughing suddenly, sucking in her breath. The corners of her mouth turned down. "My girl's gone."

Mama put down her cards and grabbed Mary's hand, frozen in midshuffle. Mary was quiet for a minute and so were the rest of us, waiting for her cue. She looked me in the eye, startling me. Her gaze was intense.

"I never . . ." she began. "I didn't . . . I wasn't . . ." But that was all she could get out.

"It's all right, honey," Mama said, squeezing Mary's hand and me at the same time. "We mothers, we got to make it up as it goes. None of us ever does it perfect."

Mary shook her head, her hair now curtaining her face. I felt sorry for her.

"No, I know I didn't do right by my girl. You know what the last thing she said to me was?" She looked up at me, the tears spilling from her eyes and soaking into the woodgrain of the table. I shook my head.

"She said she'd rather kill herself than end up like me! I only . . . I only wanted . . . to give her so much . . ."

Mama, ever knowing how to shift the attention in a room, suddenly laughed, so everyone turned to her. "Mary, I remember you working your fingers to the bone at the plant, so you could go to beauty school in Punxsutawney, *just* so you could make a life for you and your girl. It wasn't nobody's fault your Datt had a stroke."

Mary blinked like she hadn't thought of that before.

"And those first years when he couldn't do for himself, couldn't be left alone, I remember it was you who sacrificed everything to take care of him," Gran chipped in. "You did everything you could. She knew that—she was just being a nasty teenager."

I looked at them all, wondering if they really believed that Marianne's behavior was because "she was just being a nasty teenager."

Mary pulled away from Mama, looked back down at the table. Like maybe she hadn't thought about that notion. It looked like she needed something to hold on to so it wasn't so much her fault. That kind of truth was too heavy for Gran and Chanteuse to let Mary handle on her own. The sad silence took over the room, our hearts.

I don't know what came over me, but I said, "Yeah, and it's not like I'd ever want to end up a lounge singer like Chanteuse!"

"Girl!" Mama spanked my butt playfully. "You just wait—you'll be mad when I don't send you a ticket to my Las Vegas premiere!"

Mary looked at me like she was almost grateful.

With that, the room's mood lightened and again they chattered and cheated, called each other out, and pulled one another in. I sat there on the buckling linoleum floor, my back against Mama's legs, and tried to listen harder than I ever had before. There hadn't ever been a time that I'd sat like that without Marianne there, too. I never knew the three of them without the two of us. The memories floated about the kitchen like papery cards dealt from above, like they landed on the table plucked and tossed up from each woman's hand.

Nobody thought about the time until we heard the remote control fall from Drippy's hand. The late news sounded, assuring us that the world marched on without us.

"Little Girl, where's your daddy at?" Mama asked. "Cold enough to freeze his buns out there."

"Said he'd be right in," I told her as I got up, figuring she was going to tell me to find him.

"Oh no, sweet. I'll go." She got up, stretched, and left.

"Time for me, too." Mary sighed without much conviction. She looked up at me. "You know, there's things. Her things . . . Whole house full a her things."

She rubbed her eyes. "Damn her."

My sentiments exactly.

"You want?" She paused, narrowing her eyes at me. "Course you want." She chuckled. "All you do is want."

I couldn't bring myself to look her in the face. So everybody knew I was a fool. Probably always did. Fine. Now I knew it, too.

"I hope nobody around here's trying to say nothing 'bout my granddaughter," Gran cut in, looking down at her hands as if she was addressing them and no one else. "'Cause I sure know plenty a people 'round here who got wants they can't have."

Mama and Pops walked in just then, holding hands. The tension in the air stopped them at the threshold.

"It's like somebody just asked for ice cream in hell up in here." Mama tried for a laugh, unsuccessfully.

Mary got up in a hurry, grabbed her things, fluffed her hair. I realized she was trying hard not to look at my parents standing so close together.

"I gotta go. Got to get back to work tomorrow," she said with an exaggerated sigh. "Datt's all a mess—can't get him out the living room now. Keeps humming that old tune he used to sing her." She laughed a little too breathlessly. "But if he want to keep eating he better clear out the living room soon, in case I have company."

"Uh, you know, Mary," Pops said quietly, "if you need anything . . . a little to hold you over . . . you don't have to . . . She was . . . our daughter, too."

Mary's eyes filled with tears but they were blazing with pride. She shook her head.

"She know," Gran said, still examining her hands like they were about to take flight.

Mary nodded a quick goodbye, then flew out the front door. Mama, Pops, and Gran all turned their eyes to me; it took me a second, but they didn't have to tell me what to do.

I ran out after Mary and caught up as she swung open the car door. I touched her arm.

"Wait," I said, but for a second, as she looked me over, I forgot what I had come out here for, what I was supposed to say.

"It's cold," was all I could think of.

"Yeah," she said. "The almanac says early winter for sure . . . there was frost on her grave this morning. But she never did mind the cold much." We just stood there, watching our gray breath mingling in the air.

"She loved you," she blurted out. "More than . . .

anybody . . . always. And I admit . . . I made some bad decisions . . . I shouldnt've . . . And I been . . ." She looked behind me at our house. "Jealous."

She choked out the last word.

Then Mary did something else I didn't expect. She grabbed me, pulled me into the tightest embrace I'd ever felt in my life. When she let go, I stumbled backwards a bit as she threw herself into the car and started the engine. Coming to my senses, I remembered what I'd come out here to tell her. I knocked on the window and she rolled it halfway down, frowning.

"She loved you, too."

ELEVEN

My legs were wobbly watching the El Camino's taillights disappear down the road, but the night didn't seem so sinister. I could feel Gran's eyes on my back, watching from the window, making sure I didn't run off again. I took a deep breath of the cold night and felt more solid, more *real* than I had since . . .

A chunk of the giant iceberg that had been sitting on my chest shifted a bit, making it easier to breathe. I wasn't so sure what had passed between me and Mary, but it had felt real. I knew a little remnant of Marianne was still with us and always would be.

I went into the house, clicked off the TV, and patted the sleeping Drippy on his head. I was actually grateful he was here with us, the crazy old coot. I headed down the hall toward my room and could hear Chanteuse singing one of Pops's favorite old songs.

It was a slow, low moan of a song. It was like it came up from some deep valley in Mama's soul, scrambling to climb out on all fours, a song ready to tear a hole in any heart.

I stood outside the door to listen.

It was a song about a hard love and the promises people try to keep, even when they know they really can't. It had hope, though—the kind that wrapped around you but at the same time set you free.

I couldn't help but go in. Mama and Pops were snuggled up together on my bed. I stopped cold when I saw Pops crying.

As he quickly went to wipe the tears away, Chanteuse caught his hand and said, "Uh-uh, husband. Don't you hide those tears. You better be glad you have a daughter to cry in front of. She deserves to see you got them to cry, that you're man enough to show them."

He rumbled out a little laugh. "As always my wife is right—no shame in crying. No shame in mourning." He looked at me, so sad. It took everything in me not to go running back into the woods. "I . . . I just can't tell what's worse, O. Losing a child or seeing my own child so heartbroke."

Aww, man! Why'd he have to make me start sobbing again?

They made me sit sandwiched between them for a minute and get kissed and cuddled and fussed over. They told me how much they loved and cared about me, no matter what and always; they lectured me on the hazards of drugs, the selfishness of suicide—the whole parental song and dance. It hit me then—if ever M had been jealous of me for anything, it was this. Even though she'd been in this same parental love sandwich with Pops and Chanteuse and me, and no matter how many times I had tried to convince her that my parents thought of her as their own, too, it became so real to me—probably as real as it was to her—that they were not her parents. She never really had anything close to this in her house. As Chanteuse began to hum Pops's song again, I remembered how fortunate I was to have the weight of their arms around me and the soft thumping of their two hearts and mine.

"Pops?" My voice was muffled from being smushed in their embrace. "What happened to M's father? Did you ever see him again? Did he ever try to contact them?"

He and Mama looked at each other for a moment, talking with their eyes. I could see they were deciding how much they should tell me, like when I was eight and announced that I was going to marry M when we grew up. Pops finally looked down at me with a very serious face.

Chanteuse cut in before he could speak. "Little Girl, you're probably not going to understand what your Pops is about to tell you, but don't be mad. People got their reasons for the things they do, and I think you know by now the fact that you're not always able to understand them." Mama plucked a tissue from the box and blew her nose loudly, as if to trumpet in the news. I think she might've said the same thing when I was eight.

Pops leaned back with his head resting on one hand and rubbed his eyes with the other.

"We all met back when Mary first moved to town," he said wearily. "Desmond and I'd just graduated from trucking school together, and your mama and Mary both worked the tolls on Interstate 80."

"We were all just babies," Mama said. "I was nineteen and Mary just turned eighteen—oh, I guess almost the same as you and M, now that I think about it." She shook her head and dabbed at her eyes. *Thanks, Mama, for reminding me that I'm just a baby.*

"Me and Desmond weren't that much older, either. I think we all ate cherry pie at the rest stop for Mary's birthday, remember?" Mama nodded and dabbed again, and he continued. "So we all started hanging out after that, whenever Des and I came through. Then we all started hanging out separately . . ." Pops smiled shyly. "You know what I mean. And then Mary got pregnant . . ."

"We did the pregnancy test in the rest-stop bathroom." Mama sniffed, shaking her head. "I thought she was going to be happy because she seemed to like Desmond so much . . . Mary just got this stiff look on her face and didn't say a word . . ."

"Des got himself a regular route on the West Coast," Pops said. "It was a really good gig. But Mary wouldn't tell him. Refused to let us talk to him about it, either."

"All she said was that her place was in Pennsylvania," Chanteuse said bitterly. "Said it was her 'burden' and she didn't want to 'stand in the way of his opportunity.' We tried to convince her that he would be happy to move back and take care of them all —there would be other jobs he could find out here. At least give it a chance. But she was too damn proud."

"Desmond had feelings for her, but he said she wouldn't return his calls," Pops sighed. "So he stopped trying after a while. Then me and your mama got hitched and time went by . . . and you came along soon after. I used to see him once in a while on the road, but not in years. I thought about trying to contact him, but what would I say?"

"It's all right, honey." Mama put her hand on his crumpled face. "We did all we could."

❦ ❦ ❦

Pops and Mama finally left me alone to change into my nightclothes. What they'd said made me understand Mary even more. Maybe something got her scared to love anybody, just like M. I wondered if Marianne had ever known about her dad. I wondered if it would've even changed anything.

I reached under the mattress, unwrinkled the Stanford envelope, and ripped it open, like it was a Band-Aid. My eyes rested on the words *accepted* and *full scholarship.* I put the papers on the bed so Mama and Pops could see. Funny thing, it felt good, but not great. All this time I'd wanted to go to California for M, not for me. I was graduating in January, so I had plenty of time to hear from other schools. I still didn't know if I wanted to go anywhere too far from home. Didn't know if I wanted to leave home without her.

Gran's room was dark when I went in. She'd

already blown up the air mattress and made it for me; I usually slept there when Mama and Pops were both at home. As soon as I got as comfortable as I could on inflated plastic, the stupid thing popped a hole. I got up and crawled into Gran's big bed. Drippy bought the giant featherbed for her, but she let him sleep with her only "on special occasions." I tried never to know when those occasions were.

"You doing all right, Granddaughter?" Gran's voice reached out into the darkness. "You find some peace for yourself?" she asked.

"I guess so," I replied with a big yawn. If she would just let me pretend to sleep . . .

"So you goin' to that Stanford place?" She sat up, suddenly all business. "You got a thought for your future, Little Girl?'

"Not right now, Gran," I groaned.

"Well, I'm going to tell you something right now. None of this Marianne business gives you permission to stay at home and live all wrapped up in a memory, trying to turn yourself into a ghost. Roscoe and I have plans. We put enough money away to help both of you girls go to college. Mary pitched in when she could, your mama and daddy, too. We always had hopes that Marianne would turn herself around . . . maybe at least go to that community college and . . . Well, now it's all for you. I offered half to Mary, but she don't want none of it. Told me to give it to you and let me put something toward the funeral cost. The funeral that I didn't get to go to and pay my last respects, thank you very much."

"I'm real sorry about that, Gran, but—" I said, trying to get a word in edgewise. She kept speaking right over me.

"So with all this money you'll be responsible for you will not, I repeat, not waste away here because of this. You understand me, Opal?"

"Yes, Gran."

"You promise to consider your future carefully?"

"I promise."

"Good. 'Cause come next fall, Roscoe and I'll be moving to Florida."

"What?! Since when? Why?" Now I was sitting up, too.

"You heard me. Never mind when. We've always had plans. It's you children who keep messing them up! Not that we don't love you, but seemed like once your daddy got himself out the house, he came back with your mama and you. And then your M, too! We was happy to take care of everybody, we loved you all as much as we could, but now we're finally getting out of here. We only got a little life left! So come next fall, I'm kicking your butt out the nest. Good night."

It was quiet for a long time as I sat stunned; the only sound was the wind clanking and twanging all those wind chimes she had set up out back. But I could tell Gran wasn't sleeping She hadn't started snoring yet.

"Gran?" I asked the dark. She didn't speak, just grunted.

"Gran, why'd you tell us all those stories about Hannah?"

154   She propped herself up on one elbow. "Chile, why you think I tell you half the things I do? 'Cause you need to hear it, that's why. That story—mostly it was true, some of it was fairy tale. We told it to keep you knowing about your people, knowing what some before you, before even me, went through."

I understood. "It's like those old African tales that don't tell you the ending of the story, because the ending is just the beginning . . . A dilemma tale. There's no answers, just a problem that sometimes can't be solved."

"That's what *life* is, Little Girl. There ain't no way to fix it. Even when it seems easy, it's a struggle. You just got to live it." And with that she lay back down and wouldn't respond to anything else I had to say.

❧ ❧ ❧

I waited until just before dawn to sneak out of Gran's bed. The last time I had gone out to the ravine I had been looking for trouble. This time I was out there for peace.

The early light was spilling over the ravine like liquid gold. There were no more leaves on the trees. They were all layered like a mosaic on the ground, dusted and slick with sparkling ice.

"What did you want us to know?" My voice echoed through the ravine, and startled doves fluttered into the sky. Hannah appeared before me.

I only had to look into her eyes to see the truth of her world.

❧ ❧ ❧

They spent those bitter cold days at their wigwam hunting and gathering whatever food they could carry for the rest of their trip. Mine taught Hannah about what kinds of mushrooms and roots were good to eat, what they could bring with them, and how to set traps for wild turkeys and other animals. At night they'd lie by the fire, talking about everything they knew, everything they didn't know. They felt right— they had each other. Hannah didn't understand how she could feel so free and so bound to someone at the same time, but Mine was tender and giving, and Hannah opened herself to him, giving herself as well—she couldn't help it. She even fooled herself into thinking that they really were free, that the life they wanted could be theirs. Hannah almost forgot she had ever been enslaved, that it wasn't so long ago that she hadn't known anything about love.

156

One night, Mine woke Hannah by pulling her to her feet with one hand and covering her mouth with the other. Without a word, without their things, they ran as fast as they could through the cold darkness, scrambling up the side of a mountain. There was no cleared path, not even a half-moon, but the only times they stopped were to untangle themselves from thorns. They ran as much as they could late into the next day, which was when Hannah heard the hounds. Their baying struck fear in her heart that propelled her forward without thought. Mine clutched her arm, forced her even faster.

It took everything in her not to scream and tear at her hair when he spoke.

"You keep running, my Brave One. Let me be brave for you this time. Don't look back. You are everything to me in this world. You keep running, no matter what. You and me, we live and die like true warriors. I trust you . . . when . . . if . . . the time comes . . . you'll know what to do."

Mine let go of her hand and pushed her forward with a kiss. When she heard his war whoop and the pealing whine of the dogs, she had to look back, she had to know.

From behind a boulder, she watched it all. She couldn't take her eyes off him for very long. He'd killed two dogs with one blow of his hatchet. One slave catcher was trying to unbury Mine's knife from his chest before the other two even thought to shoot.

But they did shoot—the boom from the guns whirled him around and lifted him almost gracefully. He opened his mouth but no sound came out.

Before his body touched the ground, Hannah dragged herself up and ran. She ran for Mine, her love. She ran for her people. She ran for herself.

By the time they were close behind her, she'd already seen the lip of the ravine, heard the water up ahead. There was only one thing to do. She couldn't surrender, wouldn't let Mine's sacrifice be in vain.

"Is that why you showed yourself to Marianne?" I asked, my head reeling from her story. "So she'd know what you sacrificed—that you didn't have a choice and she did?"

I looked up as a red-tailed hawk screeched high above, circling. Except for her, I was alone.

TWELVE

IT WASN'T until months later when Gran's crocuses and daffodils were stretching their green necks out of the soil, when I finally saw Marianne in the dark mess I'd been calling sleep.

When I finally did return to my dreams was a warm night in early April—I'd just received my acceptance into MIT. I was pleased with myself (I was surprised Gran didn't do a somersault down the hall when I broke the news) but I still couldn't sleep. The acceptance didn't make me rowdy—it was the fact that I didn't want to go. Neither of the options that had seemed so well laid out felt right to me now that M was gone. I decided to walk in the woods, sniffing the air like it was brand new. Before I knew it, I was at our old tree. I didn't purposely walk to it; I hadn't been out here for a long time. I climbed it (not as easily as I remembered) and felt for our carved heart on its trunk—*M+O 4EVR.* I reached inside the little nook, hoping not to disturb some mutant vampire bats. But it was still there, all alone, our little box. I pulled it out, climbed down, and headed for the blackberry hedge. As I walked, I remembered the last time I had been there with M as Mlapo and my feet got heavier with every step.

It had been the summer before we started eleventh grade. Like so many nights that summer, I couldn't sleep. Tenth grade had been a long school year of M pretending I wasn't alive to impress the kids in the jock set so she could eventually try out for the cheerleading squad—only to have me ruin it for her. At first, she'd just stopped talking to me in school, but we'd see each other most nights and on the weekends at my house, and she'd be the same M I always knew. She'd look so happy when she'd talk about being a cheerleader, like it was the answer to all her troubles. I pretended to understand, to be happy for her, but I really just wanted us to go back to being Omali and Mlapo—back to her being all mine. By the time school was over that year, I was officially on my own. I tried to pretend it hadn't gutted me. To make matters worse,

Gran had enrolled me in summer school computer classes. She tried to get M to go, too, but couldn't get Mary behind the idea enough to make her. Since I was working most days at the Drip 'n' Drop, I barely had time to see M, even if she'd wanted to see me. Even though we'd had a few superficial chats at school, the connection between us was as stiff as one of Drippy's collars.

That night almost two years ago, just a week before school started again and only five months before Kourtney called me out in the cafeteria, it was incredibly hot and the moon was huge and bright. I climbed out my bedroom window and went for a walk in the woods. I found myself at our blackberry bush without a thought. I remember thinking about how Gran was surprised the first time we came back to the house dyed purple from the juice.

"Leave it to you two to tame a blackberry bush," she'd said. "Some folks believe they mean loss and regret 'cause their thorns'll catch you, hold you. Just remember—don't eat none after October, 'cause the devil comes and pisses on 'em."

Who knew where Gran got her crazy ideas, but when I crawled into the clearing that night, I finally began to understand what she'd meant. M was there, too, to my surprise. Neither of us said anything—we just lay side by side, looking at the moon peeking through the branches above us. We'd grown so big, there was barely enough room. I could feel the sweaty dampness of her skin brushing against me each time we took a breath. The mosquitoes were eating me alive, but I didn't dare swat at them. The many times we had been like that throughout our childhood, and it had never made me feel the way I felt just then. It was like all the cells in my body were vibrating hummingbird wings. I wanted to touch her so bad but didn't know where to begin. I don't know how long it was we were like that, but the sky became lighter and lighter and the moon disappeared from our view.

M sat up; I thought she was leaving—I panicked. I wanted to do something, anything to keep her with me. She leaned over and looked into my face—was she waiting for me to do something? Before I could figure out how to tell her how I felt, how I wanted her, how much I wanted us to go back to just being us, she reached up and plucked a blackberry, put it into her mouth, and pressed her lips to mine. I was so nervous I just lay there like a corpse, too stunned to respond. I wanted to kiss her back but she pulled away from me too soon, scrambled out of the clearing. I went to chase after her, but the thorns of the bush caught hold of me like hands. By the time I got free, she was gone. I walked all the way over to her house and threw pebbles at the window, but she didn't answer. The next day I went back on my bike—she didn't come out. We hadn't been alone together since then until she walked into the Drip 'n' Drop last November and then straight out of my life.

❧ ❧ ❧

I almost couldn't find our little blackberry castle in the darkness. It took me a while to find the opening, and I could barely get through it. It was smaller than I had remembered in there. I held the little box on my chest and opened it. Everything was still there: the shells from the beach, the arrowhead, and a red feather. At the bottom, though, was a piece of paper that hadn't been there before. I opened it, my hands shaking. I could barely make out Marianne's scrawl in the darkness: *it wasn't me, it wasn't you. i just got tired of this place so I flew.* I cried myself to sleep.

And just like in all my old dreams, I was Omali, running through the woods with Mlapo, hands clasped tight. It was another familiar autumn of golds, reds, and bronzes. We broke into the pale honey light of the meadow, gasping with delight—the air was full of milkweed, hundreds of thousands of floating wishes. I jumped, grabbing at the sky, filling up my arms with the feathery white wishes. When I landed on the ground again, Mlapo stood there with both her hands full.

"Let's make a hundred wishes!" I said, ecstatic. "With all these, I bet at least one will come true!" Just as I was about to squeeze my eyes shut to wish my usual wish for us to be together forever, Mlapo pushed all her wishes over to me, except one. I tried to give them back but she turned into Marianne, dressed as she was when she picked me up from the Drip 'n' Drop that day, and I had to remember she was dead and this was just a dream. It was so painful that I tried to wake myself up, but she wouldn't let me go.

"I want you to have these," she said, her eyes glittering. "You'll have to make the wishes for both of us now." She held out her fist and opened her fingers, revealing the one remaining wish. It looked so fragile there after being held so tight.

I looked up into her face and she was glowing with peace. She held up her wish. "There's only one wish I have now, and it's as much for me as it is for you. I wish you all the love that you deserve, all the love I couldn't give."

I frowned as the light around her grew steadily brighter.

"O, you know what you have to do to make sure wishes like these come true?" she asked. I shook my head.

She looked me in the eyes and smiled. She was glowing so bright I had to squint to see her form. "You have to let them fly."

When I woke up, my heart ached as I remembered the dream, but I was full of hope. The sky looked almost empty, only a few stars still brave enough to try to light up that darkness. But I could see one little star twinkling clearly, burning brighter than all the rest. I winked at it, wishing it was Marianne looking down on me. I think that star winked back.

THE PUNXSUTAWNEY SPIRIT

"Your Community Newspaper Since 1873"
May 14, 2011

GRADUATION NOTICE

THE WESLEY FAMILY proudly announces the graduation of their daughter, OPAL, from Spelman, a historically black college for young women. She graduated summa cum laude in Environmental Sciences. She will be attending graduate school in the fall, where she will continue to study Pennsylvania plant life.

CONGRATULATIONS, OPAL! *Love, Mama, Pops, Gran, Drippy, and Mary*